DEEP IN THE
 COLOMBIAN JUNGLE

Crouching in the undergrowth at the edge of the battle-wrecked compound, Rod scanned the enemy's radio frequencies, focusing on an urgent transmission coming from very close by. Crosshairs flicked across Rod's visual field, centering on a Quonset hut.

He aimed the M-60 machine gun slung from his shoulder and squeezed the trigger. Thunder hammered between his massive hands, and tracers seared into the corrugated steel shell of the Quonset hut. A door blew out, and the flash and spark of ricochets illuminated the interior.

The radio fell silent.

Rod scanned the compound with emotionless precision, overlaying the visual spectrum with the glowing, heat-coded colors of infrared. Shadows cast by the pall of smoke overhead drifted across the ground, now shrouding, now revealing the unmoving sprawls of men lying in the red clay. Most wore army fatigues.

As black, as large, and as silent as Death, Rod emerged from the jungle.

El Cybernarco. The Cybernarc.

Also by Robert Cain

Cybernarc
Gold Dragon

Published by
HarperPaperbacks

CYBERNARC

ISLAND KILL

ROBERT CAIN

HarperPaperbacks
A Division of HarperCollins*Publishers*

HarperPaperbacks *A Division of* HarperCollins*Publishers*
10 East 53rd Street, New York, N.Y. 10022

Cover illustration by Rick Nemo

First printing: April 1992

Printed in the United States of America

HarperPaperbacks and colophon are trademarks of HarperCollins*Publishers*

10 9 8 7 6 5 4 3 2 1

❂ Prologue

SMOKE STAINED THE COLOMBIAN JUNGLE SKY and hung in greasy black clots among the trees. The warehouses and labs were blazing fiercely now, and the air was thick with the sharp bite of ether fumes. Crouching in the undergrowth at the edge of the battle-wrecked compound, Rod scanned through the enemy's radio frequencies, focusing on an urgent transmission coming from very close by.

"Escuchamé! Escuchamé!" the radio voice was saying. Panic edged the voice. *"El Cybernarco está aquí! El Cybernarco . . ."*

Cross hairs flicked across Rod's visual field, centering on the source of transmissions: a Quonset hut, fire-blackened but relatively undamaged, squatting among the burning ruins. Blocks of data listed frequency, signal strength, range, and bearing. The transmitter was probably a military-issue backpack radio; the jungle compound's main radio shack had already been destroyed.

He aimed the M-60 machine gun slung from his shoulder and squeezed the trigger. Thunder hammered between his massive hands, and tracers seared into the corrugated steel shell of the Quonset hut. A door blew out, and the flash and spark of ricochets illuminated the interior.

1

The radio fell silent.

Rod scanned the compound with emotionless precision, overlaying the visual spectrum with the glowing, heat-coded colors of infrared. Shadows cast by the pall of smoke overhead drifted across the ground, now shrouding, now revealing the unmoving sprawls of men lying in the red clay. Most wore army fatigues.

As black, as large, and as silent as Death, Rod emerged from the jungle.

El Cybernarco. The Cybernarc.

Rod was neither a cyborg nor a narcotics agent. That nickname had been hung on him by American reporters months earlier, after a firefight on the outskirts of Washington, D.C. Officially he was RAMROD Mark I, the newly operational high-tech weapon in America's most desperate, most secret war.

He was a robot, a *combat* robot designed in the years after Vietnam as the prototype for an army of programmable robotic soldiers. The project had ultimately been scrapped, but Rod had found other employment with the U.S. government . . . the war on drugs.

In Combat Mod he was an ebony, man-shaped tank, two meters tall, and massing over four hundred pounds. The black ceramic and alloy plate on his chest bore several bright smears of lead left by ricocheting rounds earlier in the fight.

Cautiously, he approached the bullet-riddled Quonset hut and stepped through the door. Inside, sunlight filtered through the holes in the wall in multiple, dusty shafts. Stacks of wooden pallets splintered by bullets showed where crate upon crate had been recently stored . . . but now, there was nothing.

Almost nothing. A man in a Colombian army colonel's uniform lay on his back in a spreading pool of blood, the mike of a shattered radio still in his hand. Nearby, an attaché case had been broken open, and hundreds of 2,000- and 5,000-peso bank notes were scattered about in bullet-whipped confusion.

Rod examined the dead man's face, comparing it with photographs stored in his memory.

Match. Colonel Rudolpho Quesada, formerly of the Colombian Defense Ministry, would be accepting no more bribes from the cartel drug lords.

Rod made the internal shift to the tactical frequency. "Geppetto, Geppetto," he called. "This is Pinocchio. Do you copy, over?"

The robot did not speak aloud but generated the modulated radio waves directly. *Geppetto* was the mission call sign for Chris Drake, U.S. Navy SEAL and Rod's combat partner.

Pinocchio, of course, was himself.

"I read you, Pinocchio," a familiar voice replied. "How's it hanging, guy?"

Rod hesitated. He'd not yet mastered the intricacies of human slang, metaphor, and humor, but he understood the phrase to be a basic interrogative on his operational readiness.

"I am functioning normally," he replied. "The compound on this side has been neutralized. Quesada is dead. However, our intelligence appears to have been faulty. The cocaine is gone."

"Damn!" There was a pause. "Okay, roger that. Time to pack it in. Cavalry's inbound. ETA three minutes."

"Affirmative," Rod said. "Pinocchio out."

He took a last look around the storage building. In moments, the area would be swarming with American DEA agents, Colombian police and antidrug forces, and government officials. They wouldn't know what had happened here, most of them, but they'd be happy enough to take the credit for the destruction of the clandestine jungle lab.

The only remaining question was, what had happened to an estimated two tons of pure cocaine? Intelligence reports had indicated the stuff was still here. When had it been shipped out . . . and to where?

Time to leave.

Moving swiftly, he stepped through the open door and trotted toward the airfield where his SEAL companion was waiting. Already, Rod's keen hearing could pick out the distant *whop-whop-whop* of the approaching helos.

Behind him, the breeze through the open door stirred the bank notes beside the dead man's outstretched hand.

⚡ Chapter One

THE SLEEK HATTERAS MOTORYACHT was well out into the Florida Straits. The Miami skyline had vanished below the horizon hours ago, and in every direction there was only azure sky and water.

Congressman Clyde Rutherford stood on the aft deck, holding a scotch on the rocks and savoring the blend of sun and salt air, of warm breeze and the throb of the diesels under his feet. It wasn't often that he managed to find the time to indulge his passion—cruising in his seventy-five-foot private yacht, the *Junebug*.

With him, his flower-print shirt a splash of color against the azure water, was Michael Foss, Rutherford's chief aide.

"It sounds like political suicide to me, Congressman," Foss was saying. "Frank Buchanan stumped for you in '88, helped get you elected. You'll be alienating quite a few voters who think Buchanan's antidrug stance is the hottest stuff since sex."

"Frank is an old friend, Mike," Rutherford said slowly. "But the fact remains, if half of what I've heard is true, what he and this Group Seven committee of his are doing is damned illegal. We can't just walk away from it, I don't care who he is."

"I've seen the Buchanan Report, chief," Foss said. He shook his head. "Gloomy stuff."

"Suspension of parts of the Constitution within eight to ten years if the trends in crime and drug trafficking continue," Rutherford said. "Complete breakdown of law enforcement. I know. But we can't justify police state tactics just because—"

The door to the yacht's aft lounge opened, and two enticingly bikinied women emerged, Mike's auburn-haired wife Betty, and June, Rutherford's wife of five years.

"Interrupting work, I hope?" June asked with an impish grin. "This is supposed to be time off, you guys."

"You're right, as always, Junebug," Rutherford replied. He took her in a one-armed hug and kissed her. "You know how guys are. Just nattering." He stopped, leaning against the rail and staring ahead. The yacht had changed course and the engines had picked up.

"What is it, darling?" June asked.

"I'm not sure. Another boat, maybe. I think it's in trouble. Get my binoculars, will you?"

Through his powerful Zeiss 7x50s, Rutherford could make out the other boat, a forty-seven-foot Chris Craft Commander. White smoke was pouring over her fantail, and an American flag was flying from the jackstaff, upside down.

Ben Armitage, one of *Junebug*'s crew members, appeared in the lounge door a few moments later. "Congressman Rutherford? André says there's a boat in distress. We're closing in to render aid."

"Very well. Tell André to pass the word to the Coast Guard. There could be casualties."

"Yes, sir."

"This better not make us late for that dinner at the Sheraton tonight," Foss said, frowning.

"First law of the sea, Mike. If a boat's in distress, you stop and render aid. Hell, it's probably a boatload of damned, silly tourists who tried to barbecue on their aft deck. It's folks like that who give the Bermuda Triangle its bad name."

Foss vanished inside, but reappeared a moment later holding an AR-15, the semiauto civilian version of the military M-16.

"What's that for, Mike?" June asked. "Pirates?"

He gave her a tight grin. "Just playing it on the safe side."

Foss looked worried, and Rutherford knew why. These waters were among the most heavily traveled in the world. They were also waters where modern-day piracy was on the rise. Dozens of pleasure boats vanished every year—often to reappear later under a different name and registry, usually with a cargo of cocaine or marijuana.

And the original owners were never seen again.

In five minutes, they were close enough to make out the other craft's name without binoculars. " '*Jolly Roger*,' " Rutherford read. "Out of Miami Beach."

"Well, it must be okay, then," Betty said, grinning. "No self-respecting pirate would choose a name like *that*!"

Rutherford cupped his hands and hailed the other craft. "Ahoy!" he yelled. He could see three men on the afterdeck near the engine hatches, and two women in bathing suits. None of them looked very happy. The boat had been rigged with poles and chairs for deep-sea fishing. White smoke hung over the sea like fog. "How can we assist?"

There was a thunderous, ripping crash, so sudden, so unexpected, that Rutherford was left stunned and gasping. Mike Foss was propelled forward against the *Junebug*'s port rail, blood staining his shirt as the AR-15 spun over the side.

Rutherford turned, uncomprehending, and met the eyes of Ben Armitage. The mate was standing in the lounge door, the boxy shape of a MAC-10 clutched in his hands. "Don't move, Congressman, or you're next!"

"Armitage! What's the meaning of this?"

"Cool. Play it cool, and nobody else gets hurt." He gestured with the gun's muzzle at the women. "You two. Over there. All the way to the stern. You, Congressman. Lie down. Flat on the deck."

Wildly, Rutherford wondered if André, the *Junebug*'s pilot, had heard the shot. Armitage smirked. "Don't think ol' André's gonna help. He's in on it. Who do you think gave our friends over there our position?"

And then things were happening too fast for Rutherford to follow. He felt the *Junebug*'s engines die as the pilot cut the throttles, felt the jar as the *Jolly Roger* banged into the *Junebug*'s port side. Looking up, he saw a bearded man toss a fuming smokepot into the sea. The two women were gone, but an ugly-looking thug wearing shorts and a T-shirt stood on the cabin cruiser's fly bridge, holding an M-60 machine gun trained on Rutherford and the two terrified women. Other armed men vaulted the railings and landed on *Junebug*'s deck.

With swift, sudden brutality, André appeared, shoving *Junebug*'s remaining crew member, Pete Hankins, ahead of him at gunpoint.

With sudden, swift brutality, one of the boarders pressed the muzzle of a pistol to Hankins's skull and squeezed the trigger. There was a sharp crack, and the crewman lunged sideways against the starboard rail, then slumped in a pooling trickle of blood. Half of his skull had been blown away.

Rutherford tried to rise to his hands and knees. An explosion of pain drove him to the deck. Clumsily, he tried to rise again, but his head was throbbing from the unexpected blow. Roughly, someone grabbed his hands, first the right, then the left, and he felt the cold slickness of handcuffs being snapped into place.

June screamed. Rutherford started to struggle. He saw
someone grappling with June, saw the flash of sunlight from
another pair of handcuffs. Someone else was cuffing Betty.
He heard one of the men laugh nastily, and the smack of
flesh on flesh. *"Ai! Qué tetas!"*

One of the girls whimpered with pain and fear, and
Rutherford felt sick. "You bastards!" he snarled. "Leave
them alone!"

"Don't you worry, Mister Congressman," a cold voice said
behind him. "Nothing will happen to you if you give us
exactly what we want."

The *Junebug*'s engines gunned to life again, thrumming
beneath the deck. Someone must be on the bridge, getting
the yacht under way. "What . . . what do you want? . . ."
There was blood in his mouth.

"A great deal, Mr. Congressman," the voice said. "A *very*
great deal. . . ."

Definitely, Lieutenant Christopher Drake thought to himself with relish, this had to be one of the plushiest duty
assignments he'd ever drawn. Nassau—capital of the
Bahamas, jewel of New Providence Island—was a bustling
metropolis warmed and muted by the laid-back, old-country
charm of a former British colony.

Four days earlier he and Rod had been hacking their way
through the jungle of southeastern Colombia, engaging in
firefights with rebel guerrillas and other hostile natives, and
burning out a cocaine lab hidden on the banks of the
Miritiparaná River. And now they were walking past Prince
George Wharf, where a pair of cruise liners were huddled
against the dock like gigantic, nesting swans. The streets,
the clutter of Rawson Square, the arched-over concourse of
the Strawmarket all were alive with people, moving in swirls

of gaudy colors, sunglasses, and straw hats. Many were tourists, clearly identified by their cameras and logo-emblazoned shopping bags. Native islanders with complexions running the gamut from richly tanned Nordic to deepest chocolate hawked their wares, their accents ranging from cultured British to Scots to Jamaican and the rhythmic cant of West Indian calypso.

Drake and Rod both blended in well with the tourists, right down to Rod's sunglasses and the Nikon camera hanging from Drake's neck. They'd arrived early that morning, taken a room at the Dolphin Hotel on West Bay Street, and caught a taxi into Nassau where they'd set about carrying out the first step of their mission—familiarizing themselves with the city.

"Hold it, Rod," Drake called. He stopped to examine a tourist's map he'd acquired at the hotel. His finger traced their path, past an elegant fountain with three leaping swordfish near the palm-shrouded parliament buildings, west along Bay Street. . . .

"I believe this is the most direct route," Rod said, pointing to the left. "According to the map downloaded to me at the Farm, the American embassy lies up that hill and to the right."

"You take all the fun out of things, you know that, Rod?" He dropped the map in a wire litter basket and shook his head. "Didn't you ever learn that the roundabout way to get somewhere is always the most fun?"

"That seems inefficient," Rod replied. His head cocked slightly to the left. "Or is having fun the object of the exercise?"

"Now you're getting it. You've got to let go. Live a little!"

"I am still not certain that my operations can in any way be defined as 'life,' " the robot replied. "Living in the sense that you use it is beyond the parameters of any robotic programming. In any case, this is still the most direct route to the embassy."

"You win, friend," Drake said, spreading his hands. "Lead the way."

A block up the hill they came to an older, residential section of Nassau, lines of mansions with wood-louvered shutters and graceful, pastel-colored facades. It was more peaceful here than on the waterfront, but Rod's pace was relentless, and Drake had to push to keep up with him.

The RAMROD robot looked considerably more human now than he had during the Colombian op. In Civilian Mod—as opposed to his heavily armored Combat Mod—Rod had the appearance of an ordinary young man of perhaps thirty, with rugged good looks, an intent, gray-eyed gaze, and light brown, slightly curly hair. He was far heavier than his slight, six-foot frame suggested, though, massing over 130 kilos—just under three hundred pounds. Beneath the realistic-looking skin—a synthetic material originally developed for severe burn patients—Rod was a solidly packed mass of titanium-steel alloy, hydraulic micropistons, and over a million microprocessor chips interlinked by high-tech circuitry to provide movement and reactions so smooth and lifelike that it was impossible to tell simply by watching him move that Rod was a machine. The difference was revealed only by his greater-than-human strength, endurance, and speed, all of which he normally kept hidden.

They'd still needed special diplomatic clearance to board the Braniff flight at Dulles, though; it was either that or hop a military flight. Rod's steel-alloy skeleton made a dreadful din when it passed through an airport metal detector.

They'd flown commercially this time to avoid attracting the attention that might attend a couple of civilians arriving on a military flight. Their mission was not an urgent one, but it was important. In one sense it was a continuation of that firefight four days before in the jungles of Colombia.

Someone was stockpiling cocaine here in the Bahamas.

At least that was the consensus in the CIA's Office of Global Issues, where intelligence analysts tracked the globe-spanning networks of international drug traffic. Satellite data out of the National Photographic Interpretation Center had given OGI the clues they needed to track two missing tons of cocaine from the jungle lab to a military airfield in western Cuba, then on to an unknown destination somewhere in the Bahamas.

It would have been nice, Drake thought, if OGI had been just a little more timely with their assessment. Group Seven had been searching for that lab for weeks. Apparently the coke had been flown out on a cargo plane less than eight hours before Drake and Rod had launched their raid.

Now all they had to do was find where the cocaine had been taken, somewhere among over seven hundred islands scattered across ten thousand miles of turquoise sea.

Of course, he mused, if the OGI had been on time, he and Rod would not have been given this assignment in Nassau. Perhaps a little inefficiency, now and again, was good for the soul.

The embassy was at 28 Queen Street, on the south side of the road. They identified themselves at the gate, then walked into the marble-floored lobby.

"Lieutenant Drake and Mr. Smith to see Mr. Caplan, please," Drake told the pretty black receptionist. "Snow bunny."

"Excuse me?"

Drake smiled. "Please tell him, 'snow bunny.' "

She gave him an odd look but reached for a telephone. "One moment, please."

Drake was a U.S. Navy SEAL, detached for special duty with Project RAMROD, and members of that elite commando unit pulled covert intelligence operations as frequently as they did raids in hostile territory. Still, the use of code phrases, secret drops, recognition signals, and all the rest of the undercover intelligence arsenal amused Drake, as much for the effect that it had on other people as anything else.

He walked back to where Rod was standing in front of a large oil painting hanging on one wall. It showed men in Revolutionary War garb scrambling out of boats in the surf, with sailing vessels in the distance.

"The Landing at New Providence," Drake said, reading the plaque aloud over Rod's shoulder.

"The first action by what were then called the Continental Marines," Rod explained. "They and American naval forces landed on this island and occupied the fort guarding the approaches to Nassau Harbor for two weeks, while powder, shot, and other supplies were removed for the use of the rebel forces in the colonies. The U.S. flag was raised over Fort Montague by Commodore Ezekiel Hopkins and his first lieutenant, one John Paul Jones."

Drake looked at Rod. "You know a hell of a lot for an overgrown coffee percolator, buddy. U.S. Marines, huh?"

"Affirmative."

"Where are the SEALs?"

"I beg your pardon?"

"The SEALs. Like me. The Navy guys who have to go into the beach first and tell 'em it was safe."

"Lieutenant? That was not possible in 1776. The SEALs were not commissioned until 1962, fully 186 years after—"

"Never mind. It was a joke, okay?"

Rod appeared to be thinking the statement over. "I will have to consider the matter further."

"You do that." Drake shook his head. It wasn't that Rod took things too literally. His programming, a revolutionary breakthrough in cybernetics called PARET, for *PA*ttern

*RE*plication and *T*ransfer, allowed him to learn, to think about things—if that was the proper phrase—in a remarkably human way. The robot understood the concept of jokes and had even experimented some with puns and double meanings, but the subtleties of most human jokes, of humor, still seemed beyond his ken.

RAMROD—the *R*and *A*rtificially intelligent *M*ilitary *RO*botic *D*evice, to give the acronym its full meaning—was superb as a weapon. Hell, Rod was superb as a one-robot army . . . but he still hadn't quite learned how to fit unobtrusively into polite human company.

That was where Drake came in, playing Geppetto to Rod's Pinocchio. He accompanied Rod on his antidrug ops, partly to provide a human backup in case Rod's systems or PARET programming should fail, but mostly to provide for the robot a human perspective that was beyond any computer's capacity.

"Lieutenant Drake? Mr. Smith?"

Drake turned to face a tall black man wearing slacks and a sport shirt. "I'm Jake Caplan. Come on back to my office where we can talk."

Caplan's office was among a warren of cubbyholes toward the back of the embassy. His official embassy title was Chargé of Special Bahamian Affairs, but he was, in fact, the senior agent of the local operations group for the U.S. Drug Enforcement Administration.

The DEA had worked closely with RAMROD before, sometimes smoothly, sometimes not. Both RAMROD and the DEA were dedicated to the same cause, of course, but there was always a certain amount of friction when jurisdictions overlapped, or when bureaucrats felt threatened.

Inside Caplan's office, the DEA man closed the door behind them. "Lieutenant, I'm glad you showed up. The sod hut just received this from Langley," he said, picking up a message flimsy from his desk and handing it to Drake. "Sod hut" was military jargon for the communications and decoding room, usually managed by CIA staffers.

CONGRESSMAN CLYDE RUTHERFORD AND
PARTY ABOARD MOTORYACHT "JUNEBUG"
OVERDUE IN MIAMI BEACH, PRESUMED MISS-
ING. BUCHANAN REQUESTS RAMROD ALPHA
INVESTIGATE NASSAU AREA FOR YACHT . . .

The message went on to say that the congressman had been scheduled for a dinner appointment at the Miami Sheraton three nights earlier and had failed to show.

It ended with the warning that if the *Junebug* was in Nassau, she might have been repainted or otherwise had her appearance altered.

The message was signed "Weston."

It took a moment for Drake to digest the contents of the message. "RAMROD Alpha," of course, was Rod and Drake. They'd apparently been snagged for the detail because they happened to be in the area.

But why Senator Frank Buchanan's involvement?

Along with the flimsy was a manila folder containing several faxed photographs, most showing the seventy-five-foot yacht from different angles. Also included were photographs of Clyde Rutherford, a weather-beaten, middle-aged man with a wry smile, and his wife, a younger, attractive blonde.

"The Coast Guard has been combing the Florida Straits for three days," Caplan said. "No sign of floating wreckage or life rafts."

"How do we come into this?" Drake asked Caplan. "Surely the local police—"

"I imagine Washington would like this kept quiet," Caplan said. "There are some, ah, let's call them diplomatic sensitivities here."

"Over a shipwreck?"

"Shipwreck is not the only possibility," Rod observed. "And that would have been the focus of the Coast Guard search. The fact that Weston did not mention this when we saw him last two days ago at Camp Peary suggests that he was not informed of this matter until today."

"In other words, Buchanan just started yanking his chain this morning, and we happened to be here already."

"Congressman Rutherford is a member of the Special House Investigative Committee currently looking into allegations of illegal paramilitary operations by U.S. forces within the borders of other nations," Rod said. "That may explain Senator Buchanan's concern."

"Group Seven," Drake said. "Right."

Group Seven was a classified working group of men and women drawn from several branches of government service, CIA, FBI, DEA, and others, serving as an advisory board to the Office of the President. It was headed by Frank Buchanan, Democratic senator from Florida, who had organized the special task force during the Reagan Administration as a direct response to the President's call for a renewed war on drugs.

The Department of Defense had been on the point of shutting down Project RAMROD, but the prototype and his support infrastructure had been salvaged by Buchanan and incorporated as the most secret and versatile weapon in Group Seven's armory.

But Group Seven's operations were controversial, to say the least. WHITE SANCTION was the code phrase given to RAMROD's primary, ongoing mission: the systematic capture or elimination of men and women around the world targeted by the CIA as principals in the murky battleground of international narcotics trafficking.

Heroin from Thailand and Afghanistan and Mexico.

Cocaine from Mexico and Colombia. New drugs, designer drugs concocted in basement chem labs, or legitimate pharmaceuticals diverted by criminal cartels looking for large and easy profits. The drug lords of a dozen countries were shipping ton upon deadly ton of their poisons to America's shores, a tidal wave of drugs that the pitifully small forces of U.S. Customs officials, Border Patrol agents, and Coast Guard could never hope to stem.

WHITE SANCTION was a way to strike back, hitting the multibillion-dollar drug lords who ran the narcotics traffic directly, instead of the small-time players, the mules, the middlemen, the street dealers who represented only the low end of the drug pipeline.

The only problem was that it was illegal as hell. Assassinations or kidnappings of foreign nationals on foreign soil, military operations across international borders without formal declarations of war. . . . Hell, it was enough to make the strongest State Department spokesman blanch. And while Group Seven's activities were top secret and Project RAMROD highly classified, it was impossible to cover some of Rod's more colorful escapades. There'd been the trashing of the penthouse suite of a prominent Hong Kong businessman . . . and the subsequent sinking of a freighter in the Gulf of Thailand. There'd been that wild gun battle on the Key Bridge over the Potomac, an honest-to-God firefight in the middle of rush hour that had brought Rod his first exposure in the press. *Cybernarc*, the newspapers had tagged him, and the nickname had stuck.

So now, the U.S. House of Representatives was looking into the affair, and Clyde Rutherford was leading the pack in calling for full disclosure of all of Group Seven's covert activities, and an investigation into the possibility that illegal acts had been committed against foreign states by American citizens.

All Frank Buchanan would need, Drake realized, was the disappearance of Group Seven's number-one enemy in the government, and the assumption would be that he'd been put out of the way by the very people he was investigating. Congress was still haunted by the specter of Watergate and by the terror of people in the intelligence community operating unsupervised, with no one to answer to but their own consciences.

But there was more to this than political expediency, Drake knew. There was a final, sinister twist as well, which he saw clearly as he reread the message. That part about the boat being changed or camouflaged . . . that was a warning straight from James Weston, the CIA officer in charge of Project RAMROD. That vast area of ocean stretching from Florida to Bermuda to the Cuban coast, the region notorious as the Bermuda Triangle, included some of the busiest sea-lanes in the world. It also witnessed some of the highest losses of vessels and crews—not to UFOs or any mysterious power, but to modern-day piracy. Throughout those waters, pleasure craft were boarded, their crews murdered, the boats themselves renamed and pressed into service as part of the growing fleet of vessels used in smuggling cocaine and other drugs into the southeastern United States.

Weston was suggesting that the Rutherfords might have fallen afoul of drug smugglers. It was not an appealing prospect.

"Well, Rod," he said at last. "I thought this was a drudge detail at first. Looks like I was wrong."

"Agreed," Rod said. "It seems that we are going to be frequenting Nassau's marinas and boatyards."

Drake thought of the painting in the embassy's lobby. "Yeah. Just so the Marines are there if we need 'em."

He was beginning to wonder if they would.

◐ Chapter Two

THE VIEW FROM THE WATER-TOWER PLATFORM was spectacular. Situated in the heart of Nassau, the white tower rose 200 feet above sea level, the highest point on the island of New Providence, and gave Rod and Drake a panoramic vista across the length and breadth of the entire island. Almost at their feet lay Nassau Harbor, sheltered by the emerald strand of Paradise Island. Nassau's Strawmarket and the main cruise-ship wharf lay less than half a kilometer to the north. East, the Paradise Island Bridge stretched over the bay, touching briefly on diminutive Potter's Cay halfway across. Beyond that was the forest of masts marking Yacht Haven.

There were other tourists on the water-tower platform, casually dressed, chatting with one another or snapping photographs. Like Rod and Drake, most had paid fifty cents each for the elevator ride up the tower rather than climbing the steep, winding stairs, but their sole purpose appeared to be to admire the view. To the west, the sun was setting in gold and red splendor among purple clouds.

Only the two members of RAMROD Alpha were not paying attention to the colors.

Rod knew that red-streaked sunsets had an effect on

19

humans, but he was not certain what enjoyment they derived from them. To the robot, colorful sunsets were the result of sunlight scattering through dust- and moisture-laden air. His sensitive optics could detect a far greater range of colors than could human eyes, including "colors" in both the near infrared and the near ultraviolet.

But he had no grasp of the beauty of the sunset, beyond a dictionary-definition concept of what humans found aesthetically pleasing.

And Drake? Rod knew his human comrade could be moved by beauty, but he rarely seemed to indulge himself. The robot watched the lean, hard-muscled SEAL leaning against the safety rail as he studied the south coast of Paradise Island through a pair of binoculars. Christopher Drake was rarely moved by *anything* anymore, save combat.

Was that something that he, Rod, should be concerned about? The robot didn't know, but he knew enough about humans and human behavior to know that his partner was still suffering a great deal of inner pain.

And he was pretty sure he knew what the pain was.

"If I have to look at one more fucking yacht," Drake muttered half-aloud. An elderly, American-looking woman nearby gave him a sour look.

"Still, this is an excellent vantage point," Rod replied. He turned his optics back toward the north, engaging his telephoto vision and zooming in on another crowded anchorage.

Nassau lay nestled along the northern coast of the egg-shaped island of New Providence. Paradise Island was the largest of several small, slender barrier islands that lay just offshore, sheltering Nassau Harbor and Montague Bay from the sea. They'd chosen the water tower for the view. From there, they could study the yachts crowding the various marinas and littering the bay between Nassau and Paradise Island.

Rod allowed his visual field to expand again, pulling back

to encompass a sweep of anchorages. "I see nothing similar to the *Junebug* in Yacht Haven," he said.

Drake lowered his binoculars and studied a map, a new city map picked up at the embassy. "Yeah. How about this place—Hurricane Hole. Over on Paradise Island, the other side of the causeway?"

"A good possibility." Rod turned his head, then zoomed in again. Hurricane Hole was an almost perfectly circular lagoon on the south shore of Paradise Island. From the water tower, it was partly blocked by the causeway, but he could clearly read the sign outside the security fence that surrounded the place.

With a machine's patience, he picked a yacht at one of the marina's piers and began comparing her lines with those stored in his memory.

The checking was largely automatic. Focus on a likely craft. Call up a computer-generated image of the *Junebug* set into a window in his visual field. Rotate the image to match the angle of the target vessel. Compare. Reset and move to the next vessel. . . .

"John," the elderly woman whispered to the man with her. *"I think there's something funny about those two men."*

Her voice was so low that ordinary human hearing would never have picked it up at a range of almost five meters.

"They look okay to me," the woman's companion whispered back.

"You can't tell me they're tourists. They're looking *for something. And neither of them smiles. . . ."*

There seemed to be no immediate threat in the exchange, only suspicion and curiosity. Rod ignored the tourists and continued scanning.

As he went through the motions, a part of him once again wondered at the unlikely—and unexpected—link between himself and Chris Drake. It was almost as though the two of them, man and machine, were cut from the same mold.

PARET programming was one of the major technological breakthroughs of Project RAMROD, a means of breaking forever the rigid strictures of traditional programming. Rather than describing a task line by line—something that could never fully describe the complexities of even a simple task that humans took for granted, such as climbing stairs—PARET programming allowed the shifting electrical patterns of a man's brain to be recorded as he performed some specific task, then transferred to Rod's main computer. By wearing a PARET helmet as he fired at targets on a combat range, Drake had, in a very real sense, "taught" Rod to run through the same course . . . but with superhuman accuracy and speed.

But once, a PARET link had brought them closer than the shared experience of combat training or military drill. Rod often played the memories of that episode back to himself, reliving those strange moments when he had felt, truly *felt* the black, inner hatred that now drove Lieutenant Christopher Drake.

Hate. Fear. Grief. A dark and encompassing loneliness. Machines, Rod knew, were not capable of feeling such emotions, but he did. Somehow, a PARET link had transferred something of those feelings to the robot shortly after Drake's wife and teenage daughter had been brutally raped and murdered by members of a Hispanic street gang, a gang working at the orders of one of the men behind the drug traffic.

Was it possible that some essential, *human* part of Drake had been transferred to the data storage that served as a reservoir for all of Rod's experiences? It didn't seem possible, and yet . . .

Drake never discussed his feelings, but Rod knew that the churning, hate-charred need for revenge was what drove the man. Drake seemed to live for those missions where he could cut down the death dealers who manufactured, transported, and sold the poisons that were destroying the United States.

Rod had been struggling to understand just what it meant to be human. The concept of humor, for example, still eluded him, though he was beginning to grasp something of the human fascination with puns and double meanings.

"Never mind. It was a joke."

Why did humans make jokes?

Despite his loss, Chris Drake was capable of an almost manic humor at times, coupled with a wry way of looking at things that Rod only occasionally grasped.

But at times, like now, his human companion seemed to retreat into himself, to think of nothing but the mission at hand, and if he made jokes, there was a hard bitterness behind them that even a robot could sense.

"I can't see all the yachts in Hurricane Hole," Drake said quietly. "The causeway is blocking some of them."

"Agreed," Rod said. "Perhaps we should cross the harbor for a closer look."

"Let's hustle, then. I can't see in the dark like you can. Don't trip over your extension cord going down the steps."

"Affirmative."

The elderly woman standing nearby was openly staring at them now.

Sixty miles northwest from Nassau, lying roughly halfway between Andros and Grand Bahama, Pirate's Cay was little more than a two-mile strip of beach rising from the pale, green-blue waters of Great Bahama Bank.

The cay was part of the Berry Islands, unknown to all but the most dedicated of tourists. There was a single village, Windsor, nestled into the crook of a harbor at the south end of the island and an airstrip to the north. Between town and airport lay the cay's only real hill.

Vista del Mar had once been a vacation resort, an elegant, sprawling, two-story mansion growing from the hilltop, enclosed by palms and island pines. The view was spectacular, overlooking mile after sparkling blue mile of island-dotted sea, and Windsor could be glimpsed through the trees to the south. East, at the bottom of the hill, other buildings could just be made out through masses of tropical pines. The largest of these, called the Strand, was a two-story structure resembling a motel, which had once served as economy lodgings for some of the resort's guests. The new owners used it now for other purposes.

Indeed, it was clear that tourism was no longer Vista del Mar's purpose. At the peak of the resort's red-tiled roof, a radar dish turned endlessly, and on the grounds around the building, armed men in army fatigues prowled.

It was almost dark when the limousine pulled up in front of the main building. Armando Estrada looked up at the forbidding mansion and the guards at the front door and suppressed an inner shudder. Carlos had been so edgy lately that each summons made Estrada wonder if this would be the last one.

Once, Estrada had known Carlos Ferré well. They'd been like brothers, back in the days when they'd been *sicarios*, teenage assassins-for-hire in the drug-and-crime-ridden streets of Medellín. Estrada would drive the motor scooter, and Carlos would sit at his back, wielding the MAC-10 as they closed on their assigned target. Carlos had always been a wild one, even a little crazy.

But lately, his craziness had been getting worse. It was said that *la coca* could make a man paranoid, and Estrada knew Carlos used cocaine frequently. Was that the problem? Was the white powder beginning to affect his old friend's judgment?

Estrada walked slowly up the steps past a pair of surly-looking *cubano* guards armed with AK-47 assault rifles and through the door into a luxurious, marble-floored front hall.

Ferré had left much of the art and furniture in place when he'd purchased Vista del Mar. There'd been some deterioration: there was trash in one corner, and someone had scrawled graffiti on once-spotless white walls. For the most part, though, the villa was still beautiful. The grand staircase leading up to what had once been VIP guestrooms on the second floor was of marble, with balustrades and handrails that gleamed like polished gold. Large sitting rooms glimpsed through archways to left and right revealed sumptuous carpets, rich paintings, and crystal chandeliers . . . as well as more armed guards.

He heard shouting coming from another room but couldn't make out the words. Carlos, he thought, probably talking on the phone. Once again, Estrada wondered why he'd been sent for. He'd been at the airfield, supervising the unloading of the last of the shipment from Colombia when Carlos's message had reached him.

Estrada felt resentment mingled with his fear of Carlos. Once, Carlos would have *asked* him to come . . . not ordered him like one of his employees.

But that, he realized, was precisely what he was. An employee . . .

Assassination had proven to be a lucrative passport out of the teeming horror of Medellín's streets. Both of them had made money, both had attracted the attention of the Ochoas, at that time the most powerful of the Colombian *narcotraficante* families. But where Estrada had been happy with a fine home in Antioquia and the daughter of a wealthy government minister, Carlos had continued to parlay his knowledge of the streets and his skills as an assassin, working directly for Don Fabio Ochoa. He'd become one of Don Fabio's key enforcers, and when the Ochoa empire had begun to crumble in the late 1980s, Carlos had been in place to pick up several of the larger pieces.

Estrada still could not say why he had accepted Carlos's

summons to Pirate's Cay in the first place, two years earlier. Their old friendship had been a part of it, certainly . . . and the danger they'd shared. Once, the bodyguard of a prominent judge had returned fire and Carlos had been wounded. Estrada had dragged him to safety, hidden him, cared for him. That had been the beginning of the pact between them. *My life is yours*, Ferré had said then. *Your life is mine.*

But things were different now. If he'd come because of their old friendship, he'd stayed on because of fear. Carlos had changed so much. . . .

The shouting ceased. A moment later, Carlos Ferré appeared in a doorway between two bodyguards. He was a small man, shorter than Estrada, wearing a white sport coat that made his dark skin seem darker, and a heavy gold chain instead of a tie. He looked angry despite the smile, prominent beneath a bushy, black mustache. With a sharp gesture, he snapped shut the antenna of the cordless phone he carried, then handed it to one of the bodyguards.

"*Compadre*," he said. "I have a job for you. An important job."

"*Si*, Carlos," Estrada said, but he stiffened inside. Carlos sounded as cold as death.

"Come with me."

He led Estrada down the mansion's central corridor, past guards posted in front of closed rooms, past the stairway that led down to what had formerly been the wine cellars. As they passed the heavy wooden door, Estrada thought he heard a muffled scream, and he shuddered again. He'd heard only rumors about what happened in the mansion's basement rooms; he didn't want to know if they were true.

A large room with floor-to-ceiling windows overlooking blue ocean to the west lay at the northwestern corner of the mansion. It had once been an expensive restaurant, but Carlos had converted it to business use. There were computers lined up on long tables, as well as banks of telephones, fax machines, and other telecommunications devices. Men and women sat at the tables, communicating with the far-flung parts of Ferré's economic empire.

Ferré led the way to one table and plucked a sheet from a fax machine, a photograph which he handed to Estrada. It showed two men, both in their midthirties, Estrada guessed, and judging by their clothes, Americans. One had pale eyes, curly hair, and the awkward, open expression of a campesino, a back-country rustic in the city for the first time. The other had dark hair and a hard, killer's look.

"One of my contacts in Washington just warned me of the arrival of these two men," Ferré said. "The dark-haired one is a Navy lieutenant named Drake. We don't have a name for the other."

"Who are they?"

"Trouble. They work for Group Seven, and they may have been involved in Quesada's death. Now they are in Nassau."

Estrada nodded. Colonel Rudolpho Quesada had been one of Carlos Ferré's most valuable assets inside the Bogotá government . . . at least until he'd died in a raid on one of Ferré's jungle labs.

"You think they are looking for us?" Estrada asked. "For you?"

"I know so."

"This Group Seven . . . it is they who are supposed to have the robot—"

"Bah! The stories of a mechanical man, this, this *Cybernarco*, they are fantasies designed to frighten the campesinos."

"The destruction of the Miritiparaná lab was real enough." He handed the fax back to Ferré. "What do you want me to do?"

"Sergeant Muñoz is waiting in Nassau with some of his

men. He will meet you at Chalk's. Give him this photo. He will know what to do."

"Yes, but New Providence is a large island," Estrada said. "How—"

"My informant tells me they have been ordered to search for Rutherford's yacht. If they do not find it, there is no way that our operation here could be traced and we are safe. But if they *do* find it . . ."

Estrada's eyes widened. "Muñoz will wait at the yacht, wait for them to come to him!"

"*En punto,*" Ferré said. He picked up an envelope, sealed the fax inside, and handed it to Estrada. "Precisely. I will call the seaplane pilot in Windsor. His aircraft will be ready for takeoff by the time you get there."

"Yes, sir," Estrada said.

"You will keep me informed."

Estrada frowned, turning the envelope over in his hands. Fear and resentment warred within him. "Why me?" he demanded at last.

"Eh?"

"Why me?" He held up the envelope. "Any messenger boy could carry this to Muñoz!"

"Hey, *escuchamé, mí compadre!*" Ferré reached out and grabbed Estrada by both shoulders. "You are the only one I can trust! As in the old days, my life is yours! No? And yours is mine!"

For a moment, Estrada looked into those hard, cold eyes. He broke the stare first, nodding. "*Si. Es verdad.*"

"*Bien!*"

But as he left the way he'd come, he passed again the basement door. The screams seemed sharper this time, and clearer. A woman's screams . . .

He quickened his pace past the door.

⚈ Chapter Three

IT HAD TAKEN THEM over an hour to make their way through Nassau on foot. It was early July, and in the Bahamas that meant Goombay Summer Festival, with parades, floats, and masquerades in the streets as soon as it became dark. Taxis were impossible to find and would have been hopelessly tied up by the pedestrian crowds and processions of costumed dancers even if one could have been hailed.

Rod and Drake reached the Paradise Bridge pursued by the bleating of horns, the clank of cowbells, and the pulsating tom-tom of goatskin drums.

The bridge was perhaps five hundred yards long, and there was a twenty-five-cent toll for walkers. It was fully dark now, and the lights of Nassau lit up the harbor around them in shimmering, glowing neon. On the far side of the bridge, the festival noise was muted to a dull, bass pounding in the air.

Their destination was just off the end of the bridge, less than fifty yards from the abutment. It was close enough, in fact, that by standing on the east side of the bridge they could look down into Hurricane Hole and examine each boat moored inside the tree-ringed lagoon.

One large yacht moored to a pier caught Rod's attention. He'd not been able to see it from the water tower because this part of the bridge had blocked his line of sight. This vessel looked identical to the *Junebug*, though she was painted white with blue trim and not, as the congressman's yacht had been, all white.

He needed to see the stern to be certain.

"It appears to be Rutherford's yacht," Rod said softly. "Though it has been repainted."

"How can we be sure?" Drake replied.

"By checking the name on the transom."

"Aw, come on, Rod," Drake replied. He sounded disappointed. "If they went to all the trouble of repainting her, they'd sure as hell have taken care of the name."

Rod said nothing but led the way down the bridge and onto Paradise Island.

"The atmosphere on this side seems quite different," Rod noted. "It is quieter."

"This is where the rich folks live," Drake explained. "Paradise Island—the place used to be Hog Island on the maps until a few years ago—was developed as a resort, a millionaire's playground. They have a big golf course, riding trails, a famous casino."

They left the bridge and followed the access road, which turned off sharply to the right. The name Hurricane Hole was prominently displayed on the sign outside the marina gate. Access to the marina was restricted, and with good reason. From what Rod could see of the boats moored around the curve of the lagoon, the place catered to wealthy owners, the sort of people who would tend to be security conscious aboard luxury craft worth anywhere from a half-million dollars up. The marina was surrounded by a chain-link fence three meters high; the only entrance was watched by two uniformed guards in a gatehouse. A large sign warned that visitors could enter by invitation of the boat owners only, and that registration with the gate was required.

"I perceive a problem," Rod said quietly.

"Yeah? What's that?"

"It is necessary to gain access to this facility in order to verify that the yacht in question is the *Junebug*. However, we do not have an invitation. We could enter by force, but it is unlikely that the guards at the gate are involved in narcotics trafficking. I do not wish to injure them."

While Rod's programming stressed the need to avoid so-called "collateral damage" to civilians, it did not specifically deal with such abstract concepts as morality or ethics. But something more than programming had been PARETed to the robot during that session with Drake after the murder of his wife and daughter. Rod would not risk harming bystanders if there was any possible way to avoid it.

"You sure we need to get a closer look?" Drake asked. He didn't sound pleased with the idea.

"Affirmative."

"Well, what are we going to do? Break through the fence?"

"That is one possibility, though there are security systems in place which we would have to overcome. However, there may be an easier way."

"What's that?"

"It seems that there is dinner party tonight on a yacht called the *Too Much*, registered at this marina. I am working now to arrange an invitation."

"I don't know, Rod. I didn't pack my dinner jacket."

Rod did not reply. He was already deep within the marina's computer network.

RAMROD's designers had included what amounted to a built-in, cordless telephone within Rod's communications module, and that, coupled with his central processors, could give him direct access to any other computer hooked into a phone-modem network.

The system had been set up to allow him to download intelligence data from military and government computer networks such as ARPANET and MILNET. Of course, access to such systems was controlled by the use of pass-words and security codes, but what even RAMROD's designers had never realized was how easily an intelligent and self-aware computer could read the programs of another computer . . . and figure out ways to get around them. More than once, Rod had accessed high-security systems for which he'd not been given the appropriate codes, and he'd even accessed supposedly locked sections of his own control programming in order to rewrite them himself, something his designers had never anticipated.

And it was this facility with computer programming that Rod was now bringing to bear against a network consisting of twelve IBM PCs with a layered access-code security system . . . and all in order to crash a party. He'd entered the system and "read the mail," learning about the dinner party being given by Lady Haworth aboard the *Too Much* during the space of time it had taken Drake to say "What's that?" He'd cracked the necessary security codes within another fifty or sixty milliseconds and was mentally addressing the guest list an instant later.

And all without outwardly moving at all.

"Very well," Rod said. "We're in."

"We are, huh? Where are our invitations?"

"At the front gate. Follow me."

The security booth at the front gate was a single-roomed structure with a wrap-around window. Inside, Rod could see one of the PC monitors, right next to the portable TV on which the guards were watching a movie. One of them stood up and came out to meet them as they approached, clipboard in hand.

"Good evening," Rod said. "We have an invitation to the

function aboard Lady Haworth's yacht."

"Names?"

"Mr. Rod Smith and Lieutenant Christopher Drake."

The guard read down the guest list on his clipboard. "Sorry, sir. I don't seem to have either name on my list."

"We only arrived in Nassau this afternoon, and Lady Haworth was unaware that we were here," Rod replied evenly, and quite truthfully. "When she extended the invitations, she informed me that they would be entered on the computer list at the front gate. Perhaps if you could check your computer? . . . "

The guard frowned and seemed about to refuse, but no doubt long experience dealing with wealthy visitors at the marina had convinced him to be sure of his facts. He reentered the guard shack. Rod watched him lean over the monitor and peck out a command on the keyboard.

"You're right, sir," the guard said when he emerged a moment later. "Both names are on the list. May I see some identification, please?"

They opened their wallets for the guard, Drake showing his Navy ID, and Rod a special government employee card in the name Rod Smith, run off by the CIA's print shop for just such situations as this. Moments later, they were walking along a tree-lined gravel lane toward Hurricane Hole's central lagoon.

The marina turning basin was only about sixty meters across at its widest, a footprint-shaped lake connected to Nassau Harbor by a narrow channel. Most of the enclosed shoreline was lined with piers. A number of buildings—a clubhouse and dining room, several storage sheds, a small drydock and maintenance facility—were scattered about the lagoon among the trees. They could hear music as they approached, and the chatter of conversation. A number of people were strolling the grounds or were aboard their boats.

The party was in progress on the deck of a large sailing yacht tied up at the far end of the lagoon.

Rod's attention, however, was focused on one boat in particular, the sleek, seventy-five-foot motor yacht they'd glimpsed earlier. They could see her stern now, which had been hidden before. Her name, a bold scrawl in golden letters across her transom, was *Go For Broke*, and her home port was Fort Lauderdale.

"See?" Drake said. "Even if that was the *Junebug* . . ."

"It is."

"How can you tell?"

Rod had increased the magnification of his optics and shifted his visual range farther down into the infrared. Whoever had repainted the yacht had not bothered to remove the boat's original name but had simply painted over white hull paint and black letters with blue, then put the new name over that.

But under infrared, the old lettering was still visible. Blue over white radiated heat differently from blue over black, and the name *Junebug* was visible as fuzzy shadings in the shapes of letters, picked out beneath the new name, *Go For Broke*.

"I can read it," Rod said matter-of-factly. He recorded the image for future playback, then turned to his companion. "I am registering the body heat of two individuals on board. Shall we pay them a call?"

"I wish we had our guns," Drake said. It had been decided earlier that weapons would be conspicuous, both on the streets and to the government bureaucrats who would issue the permits to carry them. It was better not to attract either kind of attention.

Rod held up one hand and folded it carefully into a fist. "I do not believe we shall need them."

* * *

A radio crackled, and a gunmen held the walkie-talkie to his ear, listening. He acknowledged the call, then looked at the lean Cuban standing next to Estrada. "Contact," he said.

Sergeant Sergio Muñoz Arrias nodded, dropped his cigarette in a shower of orange sparks, and gathered the others with his eyes. *"Está tiempo,"* he said. "We go. Estrada, you stay here, out of sight. You could be linked to Señor Ferré, should anything go wrong."

Estrada nodded, more than happy to let the Cuban handle the assignment. During his days as a *sicario*, Estrada had helped kill . . . how many men for money? Sixteen? Eighteen? He could not remember now. But he recognized in Muñoz a cold-blooded approach to death that he himself had never been able to achieve.

He wondered if perhaps that was why he and Carlos had fared so differently.

Eight men had been waiting for him on the dock when the aging Grumman Goose amphibian carrying Estrada as its sole passenger taxied up the ramp and out of the water at Chalk's seaplane base on the south coast of Paradise Island. Estrada knew their leader, a Cuban expatriate named Muñoz who ran Ferré's New Providence enforcement arm. The Cuban had accepted the sealed envelope without comment, studied the fax inside, then issued his orders. The team knew Nassau and its environs well. The nearby Paradise Island Bridge would provide an ideal vantage point from which one of their number could watch Hurricane Hole and report by radio to the others if anything suspicious happened.

Ferré never revealed more than the barest minimum of his operation even to his closest associates, so defensive, so paranoid had he become during the past several years, but Estrada knew that much of the operation's security depended on the control of several key figures within the Bahamian government. Muñoz and his men were Ferré's point of contact with the government; they paid the bribes, and they were on hand to insure that bought men stayed bought.

In two years, they'd only needed to arrange the spectacularly gruesome deaths of one Bahamian official and his family to keep the rest in line. That special Colombian touch common to such executions—a thick roll of banknotes jammed into the naked crotch of the traitor's dead wife—had told the others that this was what happened to *putas*, prostitutes who'd sold themselves, then sold themselves again to someone else.

The others had not needed a second lesson.

And now Ferré's special team of enforcers were on hand to take care of another necessary chore in the Nassau area.

And Estrada would wait for them at the plane.

Drake walked at Rod's side, moving up a gravel path that circled the lagoon. No one paid any attention to them. If they were inside the security perimeter and not doing any obvious skulking or sneaking, they obviously belonged there. Casually dressed in slacks and sports shirts, they looked no more out of place than any of the marina's legitimate boaters.

The *Go For Broke*, nee *Junebug*, towered above the wooden pier, moored fore and aft by heavy lines. A boarding plank had been extended from the pier to an open gangway on the yacht's afterdeck. There were no signs of guards or other precautions. It all seemed quite innocent, in fact.

Junebug's presence here, repainted and renamed, confirmed that she'd been hijacked. It was remotely possible that she'd already been sold to some other, innocent party, but that seemed unlikely in only three days. Drake had to assume that the two people aboard were either the pirates who had hijacked her, or their agents.

"Where are they?" Drake asked.

"Inside," the robot replied. "The aft lounge."

Drake looked around the marina. The party on the *Too Much* was still going full swing. There was no sign that the two of them had been noticed as they stood among the shadows of the marina dock.

Swiftly, he mounted the gangplank and hurried aboard the *Junebug*, silently stepping onto her afterdeck. He could hear voices close by. Rod had been right. Two men were talking in the main cabin, the door almost within reach.

The deck swayed beneath Drake's feet and he held his breath. He'd forgotten what Rod's nearly three-hundred-pounds' mass would do, stepping onto a boat tied to the side of a dock.

The men inside must have felt the movement, too.

Drake exchanged a quick nod with the robot, then stepped to one side of the door while Rod went to the other. The door opened and a pudgy-looking man in a flowered shirt and carrying an Ingram MAC-10 stepped up onto the afterdeck.

"Who's there?" the man snapped into the darkness.

Rod's forearm whipped around in a short, tight arc, moving so quickly that Drake heard a distinct *crack* in the air. The blow caught the gunman across the bridge of the nose and kept going, crushing nasal cartilage and bone, splintering both zygomatic arches, and smashing through the skull like a hammer-smashed eggshell. Most of the head from ears and eyes up simply disintegrated, and blood, clumps of hair, and gray tissue splattered across the deckhouse's new paint job. With his free hand, Rod pulled the MAC-10 from the man's death grip, then tossed the weapon to Drake.

The SEAL snatched the weapon out of the air and snapped the bolt back, chambering a round. Nodding to Rod, he stood ready beside the door. The robot turned the corpse around and, holding it in front of him, spun into the doorway leading into the *Junebug*'s aft lounge. Drake followed close behind.

Steps led down to the room's deck. The lounge was luxuriously furnished with rich wood paneling and ornate fixtures, but the place looked like a pigsty, with empty pizza boxes and crushed beer cans littering the carpet, and bulging, twist-tie-sealed garbage bags lying everywhere.

Gunfire barked from the near darkness of the wet bar at the far end of the room, and bullets smacked into the near-headless body with cold, wet thuds. Rod flexed his arms, and the body was propelled across the salon, legs and arms flailing. Drake heard a scream and a crash as a mirror shattered. Then the second gunman was down, struggling to get out from under the bloody corpse that had pinned him behind the bar.

Rod vaulted the bar and was on the man in an instant, batting aside the pistol and lifting the drug runner in the powerful grip of one hand.

"Put me down!" the man yelled. "Put me down, you big ape!"

Drake waited a moment by the door, listening. The gunshots, muffled inside the well-built and soundproofed yacht, did not appear to have alarmed anyone else in the marina. The party on the far side of the lagoon was still going full blast. He looked back at the bar, where Rod continued to hold the prisoner a foot off the deck. Rod's gaze was hard, unwavering, and utterly inhuman. Drake remembered that the RAMROD technicians had been having trouble with the computer biomimicry subroutine that allowed Rod to blink.

He wondered whether that hard stare was deliberate on Rod's part, or the result of some glitch in his programming.

"I believe," Rod said to the captive in a voice hard as Death, "that you should tell us about yourself."

ⓦChapter Four

DRAKE LEANED OVER, bringing his face to within a few inches of the prisoner's. "Benny, I really think you ought to cooperate with my friend here. He gets really wired when people don't answer his questions, know what I mean?"

"Fuck you!" Benjamin Franklin Armitage struggled against Rod's unrelenting grip on his shirt collar. "Fuck both of you! I ain't tellin' you nothin'! You got no right to barge in here like you did! No right at all! Where's your warrant? Where's your—"

Rod shook the prisoner once, lightly, but it rattled his teeth hard enough to silence the string of panic-edged profanity and threats.

Drake looked at Rod and shook his head. The man had told them his name and the name of the dead man—André—and nothing else. He wouldn't even admit that the trash bags scattered through the yacht—each one stuffed with bales of high-quality marijuana—were his, nor did he have anything to say about his presence on a congressman's yacht, even when a photograph of Rutherford and his wife was discovered in the master cabin.

Drake suspected that he was more afraid of whoever he

39

was working for than he was of the two commandos who had boarded the *Go For Broke*.

"The stove, I believe," Rod said, his voice cold and crisp, like dry ice.

Drake's eyebrows arched up his face. "Aw, c'mon, Rod. Not the stove."

"I require necessary data," the robot replied. "Mr. Armitage has not responded to polite requests. Perhaps physical persuasion will convince him to cooperate with us."

"Now, wait just a fuckin' minute!" Armitage bawled. "You can't! You *can't*! What kind of policemen are you?"

"Who said we're policemen?" Drake asked.

"Coast Guard?" Armitage looked from Rod to Drake and back again. "DEA?"

"Negative," Rod said as he carried Armitage toward the yacht's galley. "Those organizations would not be permitted to employ the measures you have forced me to use."

He continued to grasp the prisoner's shirt collar with his left hand, suspending the man with feet kicking a foot off the deck. Armitage's hands alternately clutched at Rod's wrist or pounded against his arm, making about as much impression on the robot as dandelion seeds blown against a boulder. Rod reached out to the galley range with his free hand and turned on one of the propane burners. Blue flame burst to life around the burner's rim.

"You can't *do* this!" Armitage wailed. "It won't do you any good, anyway! You don't know what the guys I work for would do to me if I talked! I won't talk! I *can't*, for God's sake!"

"You have a simple choice," Rod said. "Your employers, or me."

Armitage laughed, a wild, hysterical sound. "Fuck you!"

"Rod," Drake began, laying his hand on Rod's shoulder. "Don't you—"

"I suggest that you not interrupt while I am interrogating

the prisoner," Rod said. Slowly, with great deliberation, Rod raised his right fist, extended his little finger, then slid the digit into his mouth.

Armitage goggled at the rather odd picture of Rod sucking on his pinkie. "Hey . . . mister?" he gasped, twisting to face Drake. "Is your friend nuts or what?"

" 'What,' " Drake replied. "He is definitely 'what.' "

There was a tiny grating sound, and Rod slid his finger out from between his teeth. Black metal gleamed in the galley's overhead light from the digit's second joint to the fingertip. The robot had bitten through the synthetic skin and musculature and stripped it from the titanium-steel alloy skeleton in the same way that an electrician might strip plastic insulation from copper wire. He held the finger before Armitage's eyes, which crossed as they tried to follow its movement. The finger crooked twice, still alive, wet with lubricant and somehow horribly obscene. Armitage's breath was coming in rapid, shallow gulps now, squeaking with each exhalation.

Rod lowered his hand, sticking the naked steel bones of his finger into blue flame.

"You!" Armitage gasped. "Who are you? *What* are you?"

"Like I said," Drake said. He saw now what Rod intended to do. "It's 'what.' Sure you don't want to talk to us?"

Rod's fingertip was glowing in the flame now, red brightening to orange. "I am become death," the robot said, the voice absolutely devoid of even the slightest trace of emotion or humanity. "Your death." He lifted the hand again, bringing the improvised branding iron toward Armitage's face.

The man shrieked once, both hands grabbing Rod's right arm and straining to hold it back. Nothing he did had the least effect. The glowing fingertip came closer . . . closer. . . .

Armitage sagged into a dead faint, completely limp, a wet stain spreading down the front of his trousers. His head

lolled forward so suddenly that Rod had to snatch his hand
back to keep from burning him.

"Shit," Drake said. "I think you overdid it a little with that
bit about becoming death."

"A partial quote from the *Bhagavad Gita*. I thought it
appropriate, and employed it for dramatic effect," Rod said.
Deftly, he reached over to the galley sink, turned on the
faucet, and let water run over his finger. There was a hiss
and a puff of steam.

"Let's put him on the couch over here."

They laid him on one of the salon's padded benches, taking the precaution of tying his hands and feet with lengths of
cord found in a storage locker. Rod returned to the galley,
where he slipped the plastic finger cot back in place, then
heated the flat of a screwdriver on the burner and used the
blade to seal the wound.

"Shouldn't you wait until after he comes to?" Drake wanted to know. "He may need some more, ah, persuasion."

"I suspect that Mr. Armitage will be willing enough to
cooperate with us," Rod replied, returning with a moistened
dish towel. "As soon as he regains consciousness."

And he was.

He came around ten minutes later, while Rod was busy
searching the ship for weapons, charts, anything that might
tell them more about the *Junebug*'s captors. They got all they
needed, however, from Armitage, who now seemed almost
eager to cooperate. Drake asked the questions and Armitage
answered them fully and completely, even volunteering
information at times.

A Colombian named Carlos Ferré was running the biggest
cocaine smuggling operation ever seen in the Bahamas. The
lab Drake and Rod had destroyed on the Miritiparaná four
days earlier, it turned out, had been part of the Ferré operation
which, if Armitage could be believed, had eyes and ears in the

governments of both the Bahamas and the United States.

Armitage never looked at the SEAL while he was talking. Instead, his bulging eyes remained fixed on the tall and silent figure of Rod, who stood at the far side of the room. In his hands, the robot held a tire iron, which he was rhythmically bending and straightening, each twist eliciting a high-pitched chirp from the tortured metal. To Drake, who had once seen Rod rip the turret from an armored car during a raid in South America, the sight was not particularly disturbing.

But Benny Armitage was terrified.

"How much did Ferré pay you to betray the congressman?"

"Five hundred K for me, another half-mil for André. Look, mister, you gotta understand! A guy doesn't just turn down half a million bucks!"

"Congressman Rutherford was your employer," Rod said from across the room. The metal bar in his hand squeaked ominously.

"Hey, keep that, that guy away from me, okay?" Armitage looked as though he were about to faint again, but he kept talking. "Anyway, nothin' bad was supposed to happen to them. I swear it! Ferré just said he wanted to talk to the congressman, is all. All we had to do was make sure the *Jolly Roger* knew where we were ahead of time and make sure the congressman's people didn't give us no trouble. Then André and me'd have a half-million each, and we'd get to work for Ferré's organization."

"Which is why you were stockpiling the marijuana, I suppose," Drake said, nodding toward one of the sealed garbage bags. "Exactly what happened to Congressman Rutherford and his party?"

"Like I told you, I really don't know. They killed the one other guy in the *Junebug*'s crew who wasn't with us, and Mr. Foss. He was the congressman's aide. Mr. Rutherford was safe, last I saw him, and his wife, and Mrs. Foss."

Even now, Armitage was not admitting that he'd had any part in the actual murders. Drake wondered if he was telling the truth, but there was no need at the moment to press harder. "Were any of them hurt?"

"Not that I saw. Oh, some of the fellas started having a little fun, y'know? Roughed 'em up some, and they stripped the girls. Told 'em they had to search 'em for concealed weapons, stuff like that."

"Good, clean fun," Drake said, feeling sick horror as he imagined what it had been like for Rutherford and the women. Armitage's straightforward account had touched a raw and painful nerve.

"Yeah, well, then Carlos, he told 'em all to lay off or they'd end up feeding the sharks. Last I saw, Carlos had hustled 'em all over onto the *Jolly Roger*. I stayed with the crew that took the *Junebug* in. We took both boats back to Pirate's Cay. Then André and me were told to take the congressman's boat to Nassau, to get her repainted. And here we are."

"Why Nassau?"

"Well, the dock at Pirate's Cay isn't all that big, y'know? A big scow like this would stand out. I think Ferré was afraid the *Junebug* would be noticed by the Coast Guard or satellites or somethin'."

"And why did Ferré want Rutherford?" Drake asked.

Armitage kept his eyes on Rod. The pry bar chirped again as the robot's hands folded it into a V. "I dunno. Really, I promise! He's got sources in Washington. You know, for intelligence, like. Least, he's always bragging about his 'sources,' like it was some big secret."

That seemed to be a dead end. Drake had repeatedly asked for more information about Ferré's stateside connections, but Armitage seemed to be telling the truth. At this point, he was so terrified of Rod that Drake doubted he was able to lie.

"Tell us more about Pirate's Cay," Drake suggested. "Tell us about the people."

Armitage had already been a willing source of information about that island. It evidently was the centerpiece of Ferré's plan in the Bahamas, whatever that was, for he'd been systematically moving to take the place over for several years. He'd purchased both the private airstrip and the single tourist resort outright, making monetary arrangements in Nassau that effectively made him the ultimate law on the cay, and for the past year he'd been working on the remaining inhabitants, trying to get them to sell out their property and move.

And, according to Armitage, the plan was working. "There's only about a hunnert of 'em left," he said. "The rest all took Ferré's money when they had the chance and split. Pretty soon, we'll have the whole place to ourselves." He took another look at Rod and swallowed. "Ah, I mean, *they* will. I guess this means I'm out of circulation, huh?"

"I think we'll have to pass you on to the authorities," Drake said. "But surely that's better than ending up like your pal over there."

The corpse with half a head still lay on the lounge deck by the bar, staining the carpet with its blood. Armitage shuddered, closing his eyes. "Yeah. You're right there. But you'll get me to the American authorities, won't you? I won't last a day in the Nassau jail."

"Why not?"

" 'Cause Ferré's got people over here," Armitage said, as though explaining something obvious to a child. "Look . . . I'll testify, I'll be a witness against Ferré, whatever . . . only you gotta get me back into the States, and you gotta get me into one of them Federal witness protection programs, you know?"

Drake looked at Rod, questioning. "I don't know. Our legal ground may be a bit shaky. How about it, Rod? Where do we stand legally?"

Rod paused, consulting memorized volumes of data. "We are not acting in an official capacity, and we have no legal authority, either in the Bahamas or in the United States," he said. "Certainly we have no jurisdiction in an extradition case. All we can do is turn him over to Bahamian authorities, together with evidence of illegal activity." He indicated the garbage bags stuffed with marijuana.

"No!" Armitage writhed on the sofa, twisting at the cords binding him. "Take me back to the States! Please! I won't last an hour . . . shit! I'll be *lucky* if I don't last an hour in those cells! Carlos Ferré, he likes to do it slow, know what I mean? Please! Y'gotta help me!"

"It would be possible to return the *Junebug* to Miami," Rod suggested. "Not strictly legal, but then, neither are covert military operations in foreign countries, however well intentioned."

"What do you say, Benny?" Drake asked. "Feel like a sea voyage to Miami?"

"Now you're talkin'!"

"How's the gas situation on this tub?"

"Tanks all topped off, ready to go. Repairs all complete. We was gettin' her ready for her first run to the States with a load of shit, y'know? That's why we were keepin' her. For smuggling."

"Repairs, huh?" Drake said with distaste. "Patching up the bullet holes? Cleaning up the blood?"

"Yeah. That and givin' her a new coat of paint." Armitage didn't seemed bothered by what had happened to the *Junebug*'s original owners.

Drake's stomach was still turning. His wife and daughter, people dearer to him than life, had been raped and butchered by drug runners. God, what was happening to Rutherford and those two women now? And there were civilians on Pirate's Cay, as many as a hundred of them, held hostage to whatever Carlos Ferré was planning.

There was a sharp crack, like a rifle shot. Drake looked across the salon at Rod, who was staring at the two halves of the pry bar, one gripped in each hand. The twisting had weakened the metal to the point where it had snapped.

"Jesus," Armitage said. "Your pal don't know his own strength!"

"Oh, he knows his strength," Drake explained. "He just forgets how fragile his toys are, sometimes." He thought a moment. "Hey, Rod? When you were checking out the bridge, did you see any charts up there? Something that would show us the islands in detail?"

"Negative," the robot replied. He dropped the broken pry bar on the carpet. "There was a chart case, but all maps and other navigational aids had been removed. We should not need them, however, for a voyage to Miami. My on-board navigational facilities should—"

"No, I was thinking about Pirate's Cay," Drake said, interrupting. "If we're going past that way, we might want to stop in for a look."

"God, no!" Armitage screamed. "Look, Ferré's got radar! He's got boats and a couple of airplanes! He knows this tub! If he sees us he'll—"

"I'm going up to the clubhouse and see if I can get some charts of these waters," Drake said. "Find something to gag him with, huh? I wouldn't want him disturbing the party across the way."

"I remind you that you are not an invited guest," Rod said.

"We're already in, remember? As far as they're concerned, I *must* be invited . . . or a member. I just have to act like I belong here."

"I understand," the robot said slowly. "An interesting principle of applied human psychology."

"Just keep our friend quiet. I'll be right back."

He walked unhurriedly off the pier and across a gravel path toward the marina's clubhouse. The building was well lit and Drake could see people moving about inside.

A shop inside the main door displayed a bewildering assortment of supplies for pleasure boating, water skiing, and fishing. After browsing a few moments, Drake found what he needed . . . a navigational chart that included the waters between northern Andros, Bimini, and Grand Bahama. As he'd expected, the shopkeeper took no notice of him, other than to observe that there was great sportfishing off Bimini. With the chart rolled up and tucked under his arm, he started back toward the docks.

A noise checked him, something like a muffled crack. Looking toward the gatehouse, he saw movement—a number of men, armed men, coming through the gate. The uniformed body of a guard lay sprawled in a pool of light on the concrete.

Gunmen, pouring into Hurricane Hole.

Too late, he realized that he was already exposed, standing almost directly beneath one of the streetlamps that circled the lagoon. Worse, he'd left the captured Ingram back aboard the *Junebug*. "There!" a shrill voice yelled. "That's one of them! Get him!"

There was another gunshot, and something whipcracked a foot above Drake's head.

Drake dropped the chart and ran, zigzagging madly to throw off their aim. His foot hit an ornamental stone set beside the gravel path, and he went flying, face first.

He hit the ground rolling and came up on his back. He heard the crash of footsteps on gravel as the raiders ran toward him. The nearest gunman was ten yards away and closing fast with a sound-suppressed MAC-11 clenched in his hands. Drake looked up and found himself staring directly into the muzzle of the deadly little weapon's silencer.

There was a ratcheting buzzsaw shriek and Drake's eyes scrunched shut involuntarily as he expected the hammerblow of full-auto rounds . . . but there was nothing. He opened his eyes in time to see the gunman spinning away to the right, blood gouting from a trio of precisely centered craters in his chest.

Then Rod was beside him, reaching down, hauling him to his feet. "Are you undamaged?" the robot said. The MAC-10 in Rod's hands barked again, and a second drug runner shuddered under the triple impact of 9mm slugs tearing into his body.

"I'm fine!" Drake said. He ran forward several steps, stooped, and retrieved the dead gunman's MAC-11, along with three full magazines tucked into the man's jacket pocket. "Let's get back to the *Junebug*!"

"Inadvisable," the robot said. He was scanning slowly, and Drake knew he was examining the terrain with infrared or starlight vision or both. "At least three gunmen were running toward the boat seconds after I came ashore. We have already been cut off."

"Damn!"

Another gunshot cracked from beside the guardhouse, striking sparks from the gravel nearby. Drake raised the MAC-11 and snapped off a burst. Little brother of the MAC-10, the weapon didn't have much recoil, but the muzzle had a nasty tendency to climb. Drake doubted that he'd hit anything.

"My apologies if I made the wrong decision," Rod said as they ducked for cover behind a large trash dumpster. Another shot from the gate *spanged* off the metal with a sound like a ringing gong. "However, coming to your aid instead of remaining on the *Junebug* and allowing myself to be trapped seemed the better choice."

"We'll argue it later!" Drake snapped. He leaned around the dumpster and fired again. Glass shattered in a guardhouse window. At least one gunman, he thought, was hiding behind the small building. "Let's get out of here!"

Leaving the dumpster, they ducked into the island pines ringing the lagoon, then wove rapidly up a shallow hill toward the perimeter fence. Drake could hear the low-throated cough of a diesel engine. "A boat," he said. "A boat starting up!"

"The *Junebug*," the robot added. "I fear I was correct. They have boarded the congressman's yacht."

"Shit," Drake said with feeling. "*Shit*! And we left that poor bastard Armitage trussed up like . . ."

"They will free him?"

"They'll want to know what he told us," Drake replied. Benny Armitage was everything Drake detested, a cowardly, small-time hoodlum who enjoyed rape and murder and getting rich off human weakness. Normally, he wouldn't have cared what happened to the bastard.

But to leave him behind like that, tied hand and foot and delivered alive and healthy into Carlos Ferré's tender mercies . . .

"Perhaps it would have been better to kill him," Rod observed quietly.

The cold observation made Drake shudder, but he had to admit that the robot was right. A quick bullet between the eyes would have been infinitely preferable to what Ferré would do to a man he thought had betrayed him.

"Come on, Rod," he said, his voice hard. "They know we're out here, and they'll come looking. We don't want to be here when they do."

"Agreed," Rod said. Sounds of screams and shouted questions could still be heard from different parts of the marina, civilians wondering at the crackle of gunfire in the midst of their high-security marina. "I would not want innocent bystanders to be caught in the crossfire."

Together, they headed for the north fence.

ⓦ Chapter Five

AT THE CHAIN-LINK FENCE at the marina's perimeter, Rod stopped and scanned the ground behind them. He could hear the enemy forces gathering—four or five men at least—and they were coming fast.

It was a small island. If Ferré's private army wanted to find them, sooner or later they would. The problem was allowing them to do so in a place where innocent bystanders would not be hurt.

"They are coming closer," Rod said. With infrared vision he could see five glowing shapes in the softly lit darkness. One of them stooped in front of the others, first examining the ground.

Rod raised his Ingram MAC-10, then lowered it. The range was nearly two hundred meters. It wasn't that the targets were out of range; a 9mm round could travel a good two kilometers before dropping spent to the ground. But the Ingram's *effective* range was a hundred meters or less. His sights might be dead-on a given target, but the weapon's stubby barrel could not deliver the rounds accurately.

And directly beyond the targets was the marina, its yachts arrayed in ranks around the turning basin, most with people aboard. Rod could still hear cries and screams from the yacht *Too Much*, stirred by the sudden firefight. His inner imperative against civilian casualties blocked his will to kill.

If the enemy came closer, though, he had a fair chance of cutting them down with short, precisely controlled bursts.

"We must get outside the marina area," he told Drake. Reaching out with one hand, he tore the chain-link fence open like a man shredding cardboard. "I suggest you head across the road and into those trees beyond."

"On my way. I'll cover you."

Rod did not reply. The enemy was approaching rapidly, and there was no time to discuss tactics with his human companion.

But he did not intend to follow Drake just yet.

Sergio Muñoz reached down and traced the boot imprint just barely visible by the dim and scattered light from the marina streetlights. He looked up, eyes narrowing as he squinted through the heavy, snout-faced starlight goggles he wore.

"Hey, *Sargento,*" one of the men called. "Let's go!"

"*No! Esperaté!* This is too easy."

Sergeant Sergio Muñoz Arrias was a tracker. Born and raised in Palma Soriano in eastern Cuba, he had helped keep his family of seventeen alive by hunting wild pigs in the Sierra Maestras. Later, in the army, he'd become a scout, and his tracking skill had carried him to the jungles of Angola, where Cuban "volunteers" helped prop up the Marxist regime of José Eduardo dos Santos against Savimbi's rebels. Hunting men—especially the wily, jungle-bred warriors of UNITA and the superbly trained Recce Commandos of South Africa—had honed his native skills to a point that had seemed like nothing short of magic to those who served with him.

His disillusionment with the Castros and Cuba's Marxist experiment had eventually led him to Carlos Ferré, to whom he'd sold his military experience for more money in six months than he'd made in ten years as a soldier.

And his experience now was warning him of a trap.

"Nonsense," his companion replied. "They just don't know what they're doing, is all."

"Maybe . . ." But Muñoz was uneasy. Some of those footprints in the soft ground . . .

It was possible to guess a man's weight by the imprint of his heel in the earth. Comparing the prints left by the fleeing *norteamericanos* with his own, he knew that one of them weighed perhaps eighty kilos. But the other one! . . .

Through his light-intensifier goggles, the Cuban had glimpsed both men briefly during the firefight. A man weighing 130 kilos—nearly three hundred pounds—would be a great, fat pig of a man. Neither of the men he'd seen fit that description, and neither had been carrying a burden that could explain the depth of those prints.

Was it possible, then? Muñoz had heard the stories of the mechanical monster called Cybernarc. The thing was rumored to be an assassination device, and the stories suggested that it had already destroyed labs and warehouses belonging to numerous Colombian cocaine cartels. There were even reports that a major heroin operation in Burma had been wiped out by this mysterious American combat robot, which was supposed to look and talk like Darth Vader and be as invulnerable as a tank.

Muñoz had assumed that the wild stories he'd heard were just that . . . fabrications dreamed up by the campesinos to explain their negligence. But now he wondered. Two men, both of the same stature, but one weighing sixty percent more than the other. It was simply not possible, unless the second man was made of denser, heavier stuff than muscle, bone, and skin.

Paco spat again. "You worry too much, *compadre*. Two of them, five of us. How can we miss?"

"Easily . . . if we are careless." Muñoz hefted his Uzi, considering alternate approaches. Yes . . . "Paco," he snapped. "You take the others to the fence. I will follow right behind you."

Where he would be ready for the expected gringo ambush.

Rod waited, twenty feet above the ground. Working swiftly, he'd found a large-boled hardwood tree above the fence and climbed it, sinking his fingertips into the bark with such force that his plastic skin was peeled back, leaving centimeter-long, black steel spikes that grasped the trunk like claws. Now he clung to the trunk with his feet and his left hand, while his right hand grasped the Ingram. By changing altitude, he'd changed the equation; there were no longer any noncombatants in his line of fire.

Four men arrived at a dead run, weapons ready. Predictably, they clustered at the fence, fingering the torn links and peering into the darkness beyond with low-murmured comments to one another. Rod knew there was at least one more in their party, but he could not risk waiting. In another few seconds, the four men below would start to squeeze through the fence . . . and disperse.

Targeting reticles closed on the shimmering heat image of one man, who crouched by the fence less than ten feet from the base of Rod's tree. The robot fired . . .

. . . then shifted, fired, shifted, fired. . . . The bursts punctuated the night with brief, stuttering rasps, as bullets smashed down through heads and hunched shoulders. One man spun into the fence with a clatter of rattling fence links. Two others fell where they crouched, as the fourth screamed and fled in terror. Rod fired a final time, and the running man stumbled and collapsed in a flailing of arms and legs.

Where was the fifth man? Rod scanned the darkness toward the south, but heat and light from the marina fogged his vision, and it was possible that his view was blocked by trees. Releasing his grip, he dropped to the ground, landing with bent knees and a thud that drove his boots a foot into the soft earth.

Weapon ready, he started moving south through the trees.

Madre de Dios! Never had Muñoz seen such speed! Paco and the men with him had not even had time to get off a single shot. But the Cuban had seen it all through his LI goggles, seen the indistinct shape in the tree drop to the ground and begin moving back toward the marina.

It was time to go. To remain here was to invite death at the hands of that monster . . . and he could already hear the eerie keening of police sirens, responding to an emergency call from someone in the marina.

Better that he should leave, now, and get word of what had happened back to Ferré. Estrada was waiting with the amphibian at Chalk's. They would be back on Pirate's Cay in an hour, long before the slow-moving *Go For Broke* could make the journey.

Moving carefully, keeping thick masses of vegetation between himself and the robot, Muñoz began working his way back toward the Hurricane Hole lagoon. Dropping his Uzi by one of the bodies sprawled on the cement, he strolled with studied nonchalance out the marina's front gate less than a minute before the first police cars began arriving.

Now that they knew the robot did, indeed, exist, now that they knew it was *here*, hunting for them, a means could be found to deal with it.

Not even a robot could be invulnerable, and Muñoz was determined to find its weaknesses . . . and destroy it.

* * *

They did not return to their hotel. Instead, after they rejoined forces at the marina, Drake and the robot made their way on foot away from Hurricane Hole, taking a round-about route in order to avoid the Bahamian police who were swarming around the lagoon and questioning the guests. They had no difficulty hiking back through Nassau, where they ended up at last in a spare room with a cot and a night-stand in the embassy.

Drake sank gratefully back on the cot. The robot might not need sleep, but Drake definitely did. More, he needed time to think. His mind was racing as he considered the matter of Rod's independence.

He'd thought about it before, often. During Rod's first operational mission, special programming had been added to the network of programs and commands that constrained his activities, programming designed to give Drake a way of controlling Rod should he begin to act in unexpected ways. Both Drake and the technicians who'd designed Rod had resisted the orders, which had come down from politicians worried that they were creating some kind of Frankenstein's monster, an artificial intelligence that could think for itself.

During that first mission, the RAMROD Mark I combat robot had demonstrated just how well it could think for itself by refusing a direct order to evacuate a combat zone. It was learned later that Rod had actually rewritten his own programming in order to give himself greater independence of action.

Drake had thought the incident amusing at the time, and on later missions he'd come to think of Rod just as he would a human partner, a comrade-in-arms with as much freedom of choice as any man.

Combat forged a special bond between men. There was something about the shared danger of a firefight that over-came every difference of background or status or rank or culture. Drake had experienced that shared trust and mutual respect more than once in his years as a Navy SEAL. Never had he felt it stronger than with Rod.

But Rod was *not* human. He did not act, react, or think like a human; in many ways he did not even understand humans or human behavior. Tonight, though, Drake was feeling something of his partner's alienness . . . as well as his ability to arrive at a plan of action without consulting Drake. Throughout that final firefight north of the marina, Drake had remained hiding in a ditch at the far side of the road, unable to see more than moving, shadowy shapes and the glitter of Rod's muzzle flashes. By the time he'd again crossed the road and squeezed through the fence, the fight was over.

So far, Rod had exhibited a self-restraint that seemed as superhuman as his strength, acting to avoid civilian casualties. But the fact that he did not think like a human raised disturbing possibilities.

What would happen on some future combat op when the robot decided on a course of action that accomplished the mission . . . at the cost of sacrificing other men with him? What if he was faced with a hostage rescue sometime, a situation that could result in the deaths of innocent civilians. What percentage of civilian casualties would the robot accept in deciding whether or not to carry out the mission? Ten percent? Fifty? Was the RAMROD robot capable of deciding to rescue hostages even though there was, say, a nine-in-ten chance that every hostage would die?

Back at Hurricane Hole, Rod had made a tactical decision, abandoning the boat and a prisoner in order to help Drake. As a result, the boat had been recaptured and the prisoner was now in the enemy's hands. Drake wasn't ready to say the decision had been wrong. He'd be dead now if Rod hadn't come to his rescue.

But it was an uncomfortable feeling, knowing that the

man—no, the *killing machine*—he was working with looked at the world around him, the threats, the possibilities, with eyes that were not human.

And Drake wondered what would happen on the day he got in the robot's way.

Estrada was a hard man, but he was horrified, *sickened* by what he was seeing. A man had been handcuffed and tied to a straight-backed, wooden chair. Something had been stuffed in his mouth as a gag, and strips of tape across his forehead held his eyelids open. There were shadows on his face, bruises where someone had repeatedly struck him.

He was being forced to watch a rape. A naked woman was spread-eagled by ropes to a wooden platform unpleasantly like a rack. One man pumped enthusiastically between her legs. Another leaned over her, cruelly twisting her head, pressing her face against his groin and bucking in rhythm with his partner. Other men in various stages of undress stood about the table, grinning, joking, obviously waiting their turns. A bearded man in military dress stood beside the bound and gagged man, occasionally leaning over and saying something in his ear. Much of what Estrada could see of the girl's body was bruised or streaked with blood, and she appeared to be only half-conscious.

His horror was not raised by the sight itself. He'd participated in plenty of interrogations, many far bloodier than this one.

But did Carlos know who the unwilling witness in the chair was?

"Carlos!" he hissed. They stood just inside the door of the basement wine cellar that Ferré had converted into an interrogation chamber. "What are you doing? That man in the chair! Do you know who—"

"The Honorable Clyde Rutherford, Armando. I picked him

and his party up three days ago in the Straits of Florida."

Estrada shook his head. "Carlos, you've gone too far! You'll never get away with this."

"On the contrary. I believe the congressman will be most helpful to us and to our plans."

"You can't be serious! That's his wife your people are gang-banging over there!"

Ferré showed his teeth. "Armando, Armando! Give me credit for some intelligence! That would be counterproductive. I doubt very much that our honored guest would cooperate if we did such a thing to his wife immediately! No, Mrs. Rutherford is a strikingly lovely blonde. That girl, as you can see, is a redhead."

"Who is she?"

"It does not matter. She was aboard the congressman's boat, the wife of his aide, I think." He shrugged, as though dismissing a matter of no importance. "His wife is safe and unharmed, elsewhere in this house. But we have been letting him watch this, this demonstration for the past several nights. You see, when we release him, we will keep Mrs. Rutherford here with us. For insurance."

"You're going to let him go?"

"Of course. He has already given us valuable information about Washington's so-called 'war on drugs.' When he returns, he will learn more . . . and he will put into motion certain pieces of legislation which will be helpful to us."

Estrada stared at the "demonstration" for another moment. The man between the woman's legs had spent himself and another was climbing into his place. Rutherford struggled in the chair, pleading with his eyes, but the man next to him only laughed and said something with a sly grin. Estrada caught the words, ". . . your pretty wife," but no more.

"Dr. Vargas is helping to, ah, drive home the point, shall we say," Ferré explained.

"I thought you said you already have someone in Washington."

"We do, we do. We have several people in Justice, one in the FBI. We even have some other congressmen. But all of them were bought with money . . . and it is a sad fact that such people do not always *stay* bought. An attack of conscience, a better offer . . ." He shrugged. "It's hard to know who to trust these days, or how far you can trust them. Among other things, our Mr. Rutherford will help us first by keeping track of our mercenary friends in Washington."

"And all because you have his wife?"

"Congressman Rutherford is a rarity in this day and age, Armando. He actually loves his wife. You should have heard him begging us earlier. That's why I had him gagged." Ferré giggled. "He kept pleading with us to ask our questions, to let him talk. But the demonstration goes on. I want him to be absolutely certain about what will happen to June should he not follow our instructions to the letter."

"You think he'll do it?"

"Every man has his price," Ferré said. "Every man, no matter how honest or noble. For some, though, the coin is something other than money. I believe we have found the currency that will purchase the Honorable Mr. Rutherford and put him firmly in our camp."

Estrada was genuinely frightened now. "Carlos, please. If the Americans learn what you have done to one of their leaders . . ."

"They will do nothing."

"I am not so sure." His flight back from Paradise Island with the shaken Sergeant Muñoz had been a nightmare. What was it the Cuban sergeant had seen over there? "There are the stories of Cybernarc."

"Which is precisely why we have need of our Mr. Rutherford's *enthusiastic* services."

"What do you mean?"

"We've learned some choice tidbits already. That he is good friends with Senator Frank Buchanan. That Group Seven is the organization behind this Cybernarc program. That they have been seeking to kidnap or kill businessmen like myself . . . highly illegal activities, by the way, for people so concerned with constitutional law. Imagine, my friend, what it would mean if it could be demonstrated that this Group Seven was operating military forces in countries such as Colombia or the Bahamas illegally. . . ."

Estrada's eyes widened as he saw the possibilities. "It might mean the end of Group Seven."

"Precisely. It would not be the first time that the gringos have crippled themselves with their own laws and misplaced morality, eh?"

Estrada nodded. He was remembering the Church Committee hearings, which had forced a considerable restructuring within the CIA. There were many who claimed that the Americans' principal espionage agency had never recovered from the spotlight thrown on it by the American Congress during the '70s.

He stared at the rape again. Rutherford was struggling wildly in the chair, beside himself with fear or anger or both. Both of the girl's attackers had stepped back, and the woman's head lolled to the side in a spill of matted red hair. Her eyes were open, staring.

"You would like a turn, eh?" Ferré said, grinning again. "Help yourself. I had her myself last night. She was very good."

Estrada shook his head slowly. "Thanks, Carlos. But I prefer my bed partners *alive.*"

Ferré studied the scene for a moment. "Ah, yes. I see what you mean. Well, I trust that the point of our demonstration was not lost on Congressman Rutherford."

The congressman was sagging against the ropes securing

him to his chair. The tape had pulled free from his eyelids and his eyes were closed.

He was crying.

"I think, Carlos," Estrada said, "that he understands."

● Chapter Six

EARLY THE NEXT MORNING, Jake Caplan had taken Drake and Rod to the embassy's communication center, where a call had been put through to James Weston, Project RAMROD's director. After filling Weston in on what they had learned the evening before, Weston had agreed that further investigation of Pirate's Cay was definitely in order. And to get there, Rod and Drake were to report first to AUTEC.

AUTEC stood for Atlantic Underwater Test and Evaluation Center. Located six kilometers south of Andros Town on the largest of the Bahamian islands, the little-known base was staffed by over a thousand U.S. and British naval personnel. Only a few miles east of Andros, the shallow, coral-sand bottom plunged into the fathomless depths of the great Tongue of the Ocean. Here, submarines and secret underwater weaponry were tested, safe from the prying eyes and ears of Soviet trawlers.

And it was private. Drake and Rod caught a Royal Navy flight from New Providence to the AUTEC airstrip late in the morning. That afternoon, with the help of Commander Charles Baird of the U.S. Navy, they were aboard a twenty-foot runabout borrowed from the base dock facility and were on their way for a soft probe of Pirate's Cay.

There was a definite problem in approaching the island. Local records at Andros showed that several aircraft had been denied permission to touch down at the Pirate's Cay runway. While there was nothing unusual about a private runway closing down—"for repairs," as the cay's tower had claimed—the radar logs at San Andros Airport showed that traffic in and out of the island for the last month alone was up nearly two hundred percent.

Drake thought he had a pretty good idea about the type of traffic that was using the Pirate's Cay strip.

The island was a roughly fish-hook-shaped twist of coral sand and island pines, with the open curve of Windsor Bay facing east. Pirate's Cay was mostly forest—green island pines surrounded by white beaches. The town of Windsor lay nestled along the bay, looking more typical of a New England seaport than anything in the Bahamas. In fact, according to Commander Baird, most of the population of Pirate's Cay—like the inhabitants of several other Bahamian islands—were direct descendents of American Tories who'd fled the colonies during the Revolution. Loyal still to King and Country, they'd built a new life among the then sparsely settled Bahamas and for the next two centuries established their own version of American culture.

Other obvious landmarks were the windsock-tipped tower for the airstrip a mile to the north and the low rise in the island's center crowned by the spectacular, modernist architecture of the Vista del Mar resort. According to records in Nassau, the resort, the airstrip, and the town's marina had all been purchased by a multimillionaire named Johann Karl two years earlier and were no longer open to vacationers.

With the runabout's throttle set just barely past neutral, they chugged into Windsor Bay.

The clapboard homes along the water looked bedraggled, most in need of paint or repair. Empty windows, many of them broken, stared like vacant eyes across the bay. Once a town of three hundred, Windsor looked deserted.

A church-steeple clock had stopped at eight-twenty; it was 1344 hours by Drake's watch.

As they drew closer, there were some signs of life. White laundry flapped like signal flags from a clothesline in the canyon between two houses. Several boats of various sizes were tied up at a marina large enough for four times the number of pleasure craft present, and two dilapidated fishing vessels were moored next to the town dock. A sportfishing boat bobbed at the main dock, the name *Jolly Roger* on her stern.

By far the largest vessel in the harbor was a seventy-five-foot private yacht, starkly out of place among cabin cruisers and fishing boats. Drake's eyes traced the familiar lines. She was the *Go For Broke* . . . formerly the *Junebug*.

And she'd been moored to the city dock.

A large seaplane, an old Grumman Goose amphibian, had been rolled out of the water and onto the jetty ramp in front of a large barn that now served as a hangar.

They saw their first residents as they approached the marina pier. There were five men, fishermen by the look of them, with drawn, grim faces and hostile eyes.

In New Providence, the only frowns had been on the faces of vacationing tourists who hadn't yet become acclimated to the laid-back tempo of life in the Bahamas. These men wore scowls, and none of them moved to help moor the small boat as it bumped along the dock astern of the *Jolly Roger*.

Drake clambered out of the runabout and snugged down the bowline. "Howdy," he called.

"You'ns ain't figurin' on stayin' long, I expect," one of the fishermen drawled. He was measuring out lengths of rope, arm's length by arm's length, and looping it into a coil.

"We just wanted to see your charming island—"

"Nothin' here t'see," another man said. "Wouldn't hang about, if'n I was you."

"Aye, Will'm's right," another said with a distinctly Scottish burr. "Thas nae damned tourists or sports fishers here."

Drake glanced once at the *Jolly Roger*, which was obviously rigged out for deep-sea fishing, then turned to Rod as the robot climbed onto the dock. "You know," he said mildly, "If I didn't know better, I'd say these gents are still holding it against us for the Revolution." He looked at the nearest man, the one who had spoken first. "How about it, guy. Can we let bygones be bygones?"

The man's scowl deepened and he turned away. The sullen, hostile mood of the fishermen was like a blanket over the waterfront. Drake took a long look at the *Go For Broke* and wondered what had happened to Benny Armitage. Was he still aboard? He doubted it. The yacht looked deserted, like the town.

Sounds of music were dimly audible from the open door of a bar in the shadow of the seaplane hangar. The Royal George looked like it had stood on the same spot for years, though Drake doubted that it was half as old as its name implied. Deliberately turning his back on the waterfront men, he crossed the street and went in, with Rod close behind.

The air was thick with the stale tang of cigarette and cigar smoke. The room looked like an English pub, decorated in a style vaguely reminiscent of Tudor architecture with wooden beams, struts, and side posts of rich brown wood set into thick white plaster. An old-fashioned, rotary-dial pay phone hung on one wall. The music, a distinctly non-Bahamian country-western lament, scratched from a radio behind the bar. Another villager sat alone at at a table in the far corner, and the heavyset bartender polished the countertop with quick, angry strokes.

Drake walked up to the counter. "Morning. Can I get a Coke?"

"We're out," the bartender said.

"Well, then . . ."

"We're out a' that, too."

Drake pointed at the villager, who was nursing a tall drink, and smiled. "I'll have what he's having."

Reluctantly, the bartender fixed the drink, which turned out to be something called a Goombay Smash: pineapple juice, coconut rum, sugar, a splash of lemon, and Galliano.

Drake took the drink. The bartender accepted his money, then looked at Rod. "What's yours?"

"Nothing, thank you," the robot replied. "I do not imbibe."

"Temperance man, eh? Just as well. We're closin' up now. I suggest you gents beat it."

"At two in the afternoon?"

"We're closing early today." The bartender polished the countertop with particularly vengeful swipes of his dishcloth. "Holiday."

"What holiday?"

The man didn't answer but continued wiping the counter.

"Listen," Drake said. "I was just wondering. I think I recognize that yacht outside, the *Go For Broke*. You wouldn't happen to know the owner, would you?"

"No. I wouldn't."

"Didn't think so." Drake heard a footstep at his back and turned. Two more men stood in the door, giving Rod and Drake a hard and searching stare.

He was startled by their hardware; one packed a Remington 12-gauge, the other a Mexican HM-3 submachine gun.

Drake allowed himself an easy smile. "I like your guns," he said. "I guess the NRA is pretty strong around here, huh?"

The two men glowered but said nothing. They took a table

across the room, a vantage point from which they could continue to watch the two Americans.

"It occurs to me that intelligence opportunities are limited here," Rod said quietly.

Drake nodded, his eyes still on the two hostiles across the room. Neither he nor Rod was armed . . . though in the robot's case that was not a liability. They'd drawn a pair of Uzis at the AUTEC armory that morning, but those were hidden aboard their boat. There'd been no way to carry them unobtrusively into the town.

And the two men across the room were clearly bad guys. The one with the shotgun was tall, blond, and looked like an American. His companion with the subgun was a Latino—not that that meant anything by itself, but it was clearly part of the larger pattern.

Drake and Rod had been thoroughly briefed on the history of drug running in the Bahamas before they'd left the Farm. This sort of thing had happened once before, and the presence of the two gun-toting thugs confirmed it.

Norman's Cay is the most westerly of the Exuma Islands, lying about fifty miles southeast of New Providence. During the late 1970s, the island had been appropriated by a Colombian who one investigator referred to as the father of modern cocaine smuggling, Carlos Lehder Rivas.

Son of a German engineer and a Colombian woman, Lehder was one of the most notorious of all of the early cocaine smugglers. He had purchased outright the marina, airstrip, yacht club, and hotel on Norman's Cay, as well as two large parcels of land for his newly incorporated International Dutch Resources, a flimsy shell company that gave his financial transactions in the Bahamas legal respectability.

He had also proceeded to evict the island's original inhabitants, by purchasing their island property, by threats, and by outright murder. The few who remained were so intimidated by some forty Colombian thugs that they fled, abandoning quarter-million-dollar homes and expensive cars rather than face Lehder's murderous employees.

Ultimately, complaints by islanders driven from their homes led to an investigation . . . and one of the drug war's few victories at that point. Eventually—and after a losing battle against the Bahamian government itself, which was deeply implicated in the goings-on at Norman's Cay— Carlos Lehder had been arrested, tried, and convicted and, in 1988, he'd been given the maximum sentence possible: life without parole plus 135 years.

But years later, Norman's Cay had still not recovered. It was a ghost island surrounded by the wreckage of boats and light aircraft that had gone down during the years when it was a major transshipment point for cocaine from Colombia bound for the United States.

And if Lehder was gone, Drake knew that there were more than enough vicious and amoral sharks, ambitious monsters in human skins, ready to take Lehder's place.

Records at the U.S. embassy in Nassau showed that there'd been complaints by American nationals living on Pirate's Cay, families threatened at gunpoint or warned to leave. Johann Karl, the millionaire who had purchased much of the island, was rumored to be an international developer planning a major new resort, but there were no indications that his plans were being carried out.

It was Norman's Cay all over again. This time, however, the bad guys would be careful to observe the legalities . . . and to purchase the right people within the Bahamian government. In the Norman's Cay incident, the scandal had touched the prime minister of the Bahamas.

How far did the rot extend *this* time?

Drake looked into the eyes of the two armed men in the bar. The townspeople's hostility might mean they'd been corrupted by whoever was behind the takeover. More likely, though, they were acting under duress. These two, however, were the enemy . . . the *real* enemy.

Drake set his drink down, half-finished. "You're right, Rod," he said. Those gunmen were perfectly capable of opening fire here, in the town . . . and civilians might be hurt. "We've seen all we need to see. Let's go."

The gunmen followed, sauntering after them toward the dock. The fishermen were still there, as was, Drake was relieved to see, the speedboat.

"Don't come back," the blond man with the shotgun said. "Around here, we eat your kind for breakfast."

"Oh?" Drake said innocently. "And what kind is that?"

The Latino grinned malevolently. "Gringo pussies," he said.

"Then it's lucky for us it's past lunchtime," Drake said, signaling Rod to cast off. He slipped the ignition key in the starter and turned it. The engine thrummed to life and he put the throttle in reverse, gently backing from the dock.

Every muscle, every nerve was taut. The bad guys could open up on them now from the dock and kill them both, but Drake suspected that they would rather do it without witnesses . . . even men as cowed as these.

Nevertheless, he scarcely breathed until they were a couple of hundred yards out, well beyond the effective range for either the shotgun or the SMG.

"You were awfully quiet back there," Drake said as the runabout sped beyond the point of land marking the entrance to the bay.

Rod turned his eyes away, toward the turquoise horizon. He actually seemed embarrassed. "I fear that nothing in my PARET programming prepared me for conversations in seaport bars," Rod said. "I was uncertain how best to proceed."

"Well, you were right about leaving. We weren't going to learn anything there."

"I also calculated a high probability that the armed men were awaiting further reinforcements. Had more gunmen arrived, the likelihood of an attack would have increased significantly. Innocent lives would have been jeopardized."

"My thoughts exactly." Drake spun the boat's wheel, angling them north. The green forest and white sand of the beach edging the eastern coastline of Pirate's Cay slid past a hundred meters to port.

"May I ask what your current plan of action is?" Rod asked.

Drake grinned. "I thought I'd like a closer look at the air-field," he said. "What kind of planes there are . . . how many guards."

"You are contemplating a raid?"

"Damn straight I am. Those people back there were in trouble."

"How can you be certain? I detected definite evidence of stress in their speech tones and patterns, but it is possible that they are working in concert with the enemy. The stress could be explained by a reasonable fear of discovery."

"Maybe," Drake agreed. "I thought of that, too. But my gut feeling is that those men, every one of them, were scared. And did you notice? There were no women or children around."

The robot hesitated. "This is unusual?"

"For a small village? Yeah, it's unusual. A town like that has families, Rod. Men, women, and children. All we saw was a handful of men. Young men. I think their families are being held hostage somewhere, against their good behavior."

"That had not occurred to me."

Maybe, Drake thought, human beings still had a few advantages over robots. Because he was dead certain that he was right.

The only problem now, though, was what to do about it.

Twenty minutes later, they grounded the runabout on the sandy bottom just off the forest-backed beach of a shallow cove. The trees sheltered them from watchers up at the resort; according to the chart, the airstrip and its attendant buildings lay to the west, beyond the stand of island pines that formed the spine of Pirate's Cay.

The surf was gentle, a rhythmic ebb and flow of foot-high waves that broke around their feet as they tied the speedboat to a sand-locked twist of driftwood. "Do you want weapons?" Rod asked.

"Not just yet. That'd be an open invitation for the bad guys to open fire if they saw us. Besides . . ."

He stopped as the sound of an engine reached them from across the low dunes at the top of the beach. Seconds later, a Land Rover pulled into view and four men piled out, all of them armed.

Two were from the bar in Windsor, the tall blond American and the guy with the Mexican subgun. The other two were latinos wearing mismatched pieces of military uniforms, one with an m-16 assault rifle and the other with a mac-10.

"Halt!" the man with the assault rifle cried, gesturing with the weapon. "You are under arrest for trespassing!"

Drake froze. Their Uzis were out of reach in the boat.

"Trespassing's a real serious offense hereabouts," the blond American added ominously. "You'll have to come with us to see the Chief."

"Actually, that is not necessary," Rod said. The calm of his voice seemed ridiculous under the circumstances. "Pirate's Cay is legally under the jurisdiction of the governor-general of the Bahamas and the prime minister, rather than of this chief you mention. Furthermore, Bahamian law specifically prohibits ownership of land below the high-tide mark." Rod pointed to the uneven line of encrusted salt, shells, and seaweed that outlined the high-water mark further up the beach. "We are not on private property."

"So, a legal beagle," the man with the M-16 said. He swung the muzzle of his weapon toward Rod.

"Fresco, compadre, fresco," the thug with the Ingram cautioned. *"El Jefé* said to keep everything low-profile. . . ."

"Sure," Drake said, picking up on Rod's argument. "We've got every right to be here." Spying a flash of brilliant pink and ocher on the wet sand, he took a few steps, stooped, and picked up a conch shell the size of his head. It was heavy, the animal that had grown the shell still residing within, the pink-rimmed aperture of the shell sealed by the creature's blade-shaped foot. "See? We're just out hunting for shells." He tossed it to Rod, who snatched it from the air.

"Queen conch," Rod observed, looking at the delicate lip and whorls. *"Strombus gigas.* It is still living."

Drake was continually amazed at the reach of Rod's arcane knowledge. "Okay," he said. He exchanged a quick glance with Rod, nodding slightly. "So I have this thing for conch chowder."

"You've got your fuckin' shell," the man with the HM-3 said. The gunmen were crowding closer now. *Too* close to cover the two of them properly. "Now beat it. And don't give us any shit about bein' allowed on the beach, 'cause you two could just disappear out here and no one would be the wiser." He shifted his aim to Drake, eyes narrowing. "In fact, that might not be a bad idea at all. . . ."

⚡ Chapter Seven

ROD CAUGHT DRAKE'S almost imperceptible nod and knew that the SEAL was ready. The gunman's finger was tightening on the trigger of the HM-3.

The robot's reaction time was *very* fast, and the decision was made within a millisecond. Rod's arm *blurred*, and there was a whipcrack of splitting air as the conch shell squarely struck the subgunner's face, exploding skull and brains in a vivid splatter of red.

Drake's foot snapped out in the same instant, crunching into the hand of the M-16 gunner where it curled around his rifle's foregrip. At the same time, Rod took two steps forward, his left hand snatching the barrel of the blond man's shotgun, then wrenching up and back. The man's finger closed on the trigger in an involuntary reflex as the barrel bent sharply with a high-pitched squeak of folding metal.

There was a shattering explosion as a 12-gauge shell exploded in the weapon's breech. Bits of metal whirred through the air as the shotgun's stock separated from the barrel, and the blond man shrieked and clawed at his face.

The last man, clutching his MAC-10 close against his chest, instinctively ducked when the 12-gauge exploded. Still grasping the shattered, eighteen-inch barrel of the shotgun by its folded-back muzzle, Rod advanced with the metal shaft extended like a rapier. He lunged, punching the jagged steel flower at the barrel's breech end into the man's throat. With a gurgled scream, the man flopped onto the sand, a bright crimson, arterial spurt geysering from a tear beneath the angle of his jaw.

The blond man rose to his knees, eyes blinking in a face torn and bloodied by chips of flying steel, blackened by burning powder. He was scrabbling for a Browning Hi-power in its belt holster. Rod, still holding the improvised rapier, lunged again, punching through the man's sternum with a sickening crunch, convulsing him where he knelt. Blood from the ragged hole where his heart had been gushed out onto the sand.

Rod spun, ready to continue the fight, but Drake's man was dead, killed by a fist-heel driven into his nose hard enough to shatter cartilage and drive the shards into the brain. The throat-torn man continued to writhe on the ground, his heels gouging trenches in the wet sand.

Drake knelt at his side. There was blood everywhere. Rod watched as the SEAL probed the wound with his fingers, trying to stem the deadly pulse of blood.

"Who do you work for?" Drake asked. The man was still conscious, his eyes wide open and terrified.

"Ghh . . . gug . . ."

"We will see to it that you get to a doctor," Drake continued. "Tell us who your boss is."

The man tried again, but the words came out a gargle. Drake was still probing, his hands now slick with blood, making him look as though he were wearing bright red gloves.

"Ferré . . ." the man managed at last. "Carlos . . . Ferré . . ."

"How many men does he have?" But the wounded man's eyes were already turning glassy. The wound spurted crimson twice more, but weakly, the jets scarcely reaching the water's edge.

Then the pulse ceased.

"Four up, four down," Drake said quietly. He walked a few feet out into the surf, then bent down to wash the blood off his hands.

"What do we do now? These four will soon be missed."

"Actually, that guy had a pretty good idea," Drake said, pointing toward the man with only a shattered, bloody ruin where his head had been. "We'll make them disappear. It may be some time before this Ferré and his gangsters figure out what happened."

Rod walked over to the headless corpse. The conch, protected by its hard shell and unhurt by its brief but violent flight, was trying to bury its way into the wet sand amid the splatter of blood and pulped tissue that had recently been the back of a man's head. Gently, he picked the sea animal up, walked with it back down the beach, and tossed it a little way out into the surf.

He was not sure why he did so, and the not knowing made him feel . . . incomplete. And unprotected.

Conflicting emotions, *feelings* surged within him. He was not human, could never be human. Why, then, did he feel this way? How could he *feel* at all?

There had been tremendous satisfaction in killing the scum that had been terrorizing an entire island, he realized, a satisfaction far greater than the usual sense of successful well-being he felt in the completion of a programmed task.

It felt *good*.

Drake looked at him uncertainly. "Rod? You okay?"

"Functions normal," the robot said slowly. "But perhaps you could say that I conked him a good one."

Drake closed his eyes and uttered a low, pained groan.

Rod smiled almost shyly, knowing that the response could best be explained as praise for a particularly witty pun. Perhaps he was beginning to get the hang of humor, after all.

"Come on, Rod," Drake said. "Gather up the weapons . . .

then help me load these stiffs in the boat. The tide'll come in and take care of the blood, and no one will know what's happened to them. It might unsettle the others."

"Affirmative," Rod replied. "Psychological warfare."

He tried to ignore his feelings as they worked.

Carlos Ferré looked up from the burned and mangled, stretched-out body of Benjamin Franklin Armitage. "I don't think this *gringo huevón* is going to tell us anything more," he said.

They were standing on either side of the big wooden table in the interrogation room, the same table where they'd had the American girl the night before. The room was small, stone-walled, and thick with the cloying stink of burned meat, the coppery tang of blood. Maxmilliano Vargas, Ferré's chief interrogator, untied the leather apron he wore. "One can only push a patient so far. Then it becomes unproductive."

Muñoz shook his head slowly. "But his information corroborates what I saw on Paradise Island. The *norteamericanos* do, indeed, have a combat robot of remarkable power and ability. And they have sent it here, hunting *us*."

"It is still unbelievable," Ferré said. "Incredible." He reached down and slapped Armitage lightly on the cheek. "What do you say, Benny? Was this robot hunting me?"

The eyes were staring horrors, rimmed with blood. Armitage opened his mouth, his tongue working between parched lips, but no sound came out. Ferré shook his head, miming sadness. Armitage had actually cracked the table with his head at one point and managed to knock himself out to escape the pain of what was happening to his crotch at the time. The poor bastard hadn't been quite right since.

"Shall I put him down?" Vargas offered. He might have been a vet discussing a sick dog.

Ferré considered the question. Armitage had actually talked to the thing, had been touched by it. He shuddered. "No. I might have further questions later. In any case, this, this *hijueputa* is responsible for telling the Americans where we were. We will leave him alone for a time, the better to contemplate his sins."

The staring eyes locked with his, wells of pleading and pain.

"I should stay with him, Señor Ferré," Vargas said. "If you wish him to stay alive, it is vital that he not go into shock."

"*Bueno.* See to it."

Outside the interrogation room, Ferré questioned Muñoz as they walked down a hallway toward the stairs going up to the main level of the hacienda.

"I am trying to form a coherent picture of this American superweapon," he told Muñoz. "The picture is growing clearer, I think."

"Yes, sir?"

"We have separate reports." He ticked them off on his fingers. "From our men at the lab in Colombia. A black giant who could not be destroyed. From Armitage. Something that looked like a man but made of black steel inside, and strong enough to bend iron bars. And from you. Something like a man, but extremely heavy, perhaps one hundred thirty kilos."

"I think we can discount the black giant," Muñoz said as they started up the steps. "What I saw was nothing like that. Our people may have been exaggerating."

"My thoughts exactly. What we must do, my friend, is assume that this robot will come to this island, now that it knows we are here."

"And? . . ."

"We need to build a trap. Something which even this Cybernarc, with all its strength and speed, could not avoid."

"You have an idea, *mi Jefé?*"

"The beginnings of one, perhaps. *Digamé*, these footprints you saw. Do you think that this robot was so heavy it might have become stuck in the mud?"

"The ground was only soft, Señor Ferré, not muddy. But it is possible. I do not think such a creature could swim if he fell into the water."

"*Bueno*. Suppose we were to try this. . . ."

They strolled in the villa's garden as Ferré unfolded his plan.

"I don't like it, Rod," Drake said. "You're taking too much on yourself."

"We need additional intelligence on the island," Rod said calmly. "We do not yet know the number of men Ferré has on the island, or their disposition. We have not seen the villa, nor do we know what kind of defenses he may have employed. Perhaps most important, if your theory that he is holding women and children hostage is correct, it is imperative that we know where they are being held and how many men he has watching them."

"But you can't do all of that yourself!"

"On the contrary," Rod replied. "I can. And I can do so more efficiently if I go alone."

Drake threw up his hands and turned away in disgust. At the other end of the conference table, Commander Baird studied the interior of his coffee mug with keen interest.

A conference-phone speaker sat in the center of the table. "Rod, are you sure you could operate effectively without a backup?" James Weston's voice said from the speaker, his voice sounding curiously flat as it came through the security scrambler. The conference phone had been set up with scrambler and a direct satellite relay so that Weston, now in his CIA office in Langley, Virginia, could sit in on the session.

"Affirmative," Rod said, answering Weston's question. "Human assets, however efficient or well trained, would only hamper my movement and limit my chances for success."

Baird made a strangled noise and looked away. He obviously was still having some trouble accepting the idea of an intelligent robot who made his own decisions.

Rod and Drake had returned to AUTEC late that afternoon. By that time, Rod had formulated a plan of his own. He would immediately return alone to Pirate's Cay, lightly armed but carrying a powerful backpack radio with which he could stay in touch with Drake at AUTEC. It was his intention to go in alone, traveling light and fast. Once he had the necessary data on the island's defenses, he would exfiltrate in the boat . . . or radio for a pickup, whichever seemed best at the time.

Drake closed his eyes. "Rod, if this mess is as big as we think it is, you can't go in by yourself. You can't!"

"In Burma, the two of us faced a much larger force."

"Yeah, but we had the whole damned jungle to hide in, and we wound up getting local help. You'll be on your own in there, fella. We don't know if the locals can help us, or even if they want to. I say we wait for a SEAL team to come in and do the Sneaky Pete stuff."

"I respectfully disagree. I can move far more quickly and quietly than a large party of men. My operational decisions need not be restricted by the presence of friendly forces. It is simply common sense to use the proper tool for a given job, and *only* the proper tool, do you not agree?"

"You're not a *tool.* . . ."

"Regardless, I do not intend a confrontation with enemy forces during this mission. I will remain out of sight and will engage in combat only when immediately necessary to preserve operational security. Additional firepower will not only be unnecessary, it will be counterproductive."

"Mr. Weston?" Drake asked. "Can you talk any sense into this steel-headed robot of yours? Tell him we can't risk a two-billion-dollar investment by sending him onto that island by himself."

There was a long silence. Static somewhere on the scrambled line hissed and popped.

"Chris," Weston said at last. "I appreciate your concern. But the situation here is serious. If we don't use our assets, *all* our assets, we might as well not have them at all."

"You can't talk about Rod as if he's an—"

"Drake, *you* are one of my assets, and I would use you the same damned way if I had to. Listen to me. I agree with your assessment of Pirate's Cay. It sounds like Norman's Cay all over again. But there's more to it than that. You know, Carlos Lehder was the first smuggler to stop dealing in kilos of cocaine and start dealing in tons. God knows what kind of volume Ferré is going to be handling through Pirate's Cay. We were expecting two *tons* at Miritiparaná. It could be colossal."

"I'm sure the DEA and the Coast Guard are up to stopping it, Mr. Weston."

"They *have* been on it . . . and for about six months, damn little cocaine has been getting through. There've been some major seizures lately, and street prices on coke are way up. We think that Ferré may be stockpiling cocaine down there by the ton, that he hasn't been able to ship any through for fear of having it picked up. But now, sources here in the States say . . . they say the word on the street is that supplies are going to be coming through soon, and big time. Our guess here is that Ferré has something sneaky planned. What we don't know is how he's planning on getting the stuff through." There was another long pause. "Two points. We have to know how Ferré is planning on bringing the coke into the States. Ideally, we'd like to know where he's bringing it in, as well as how."

"And the second point?" Drake asked.

"If this Pirate's Cay operation is as big and as bad as you say it is, we're going to need a major operation to clean it out. I'll agree with you there, Lieutenant. You and Rod won't be able to take it on by yourselves. We'll need a small army."

Commander Baird cleared his throat. "Ah . . . if it's any help, Mr. Weston," he said. "I have sixty U.S. Marines here on the base, attached to my security department. I'm sure they wouldn't mind a little combat deployment as a way of breaking the monotony of guarding the pier."

"Thank you, Commander. I'll keep that in mind. In any case, we're going to have to open negotiations with Nassau. Can't go running off half-cocked with illegal military deployments on their territory, you know. But it strikes me the deployment is going to have to be out of the AUTEC facility. It'll be easier operating out of there than from Florida."

"We're ready and able, Mr. Weston," Baird said.

"Thank you, Commander." Weston paused. "Rod, I'm approving your recce. Code name SEA KING."

"SEA KING," Rod repeated.

"Get onto the island. Carry out your reconnaissance. See what you can learn about their strength, their disposition. But I especially want to know what you can learn about their smuggling operation. Anything that's supposed to bring in tons and tons of cocaine has to be pretty big. Keep your optics peeled for . . . for whatever it might be."

" 'Optics peeled,' " Rod repeated. He seemed to puzzle over the phrase for a moment. "I shall remain alert."

"As of now, Carlos Ferré is on the WHITE SANCTION list. Do you understand?"

"Affirmative."

"Good. One way or the other, we shut that bastard down. Chris? You have anything to add?"

Drake hesitated.

"Lieutenant?" Weston's voice prompted. "You have doubts?"

Drake glanced at Rod, who was seated impassively at his side. "Not doubts, exactly. But I think Rod should have some backup. He shouldn't go in alone."

There was a long pause. "I think this time I'll have to rule with Rod, son. He can do this better without you. And I need you at AUTEC."

"Yes, sir. May I ask why?"

"This is going to be a big operation. The negotiations with the Bahamian parliament are going to be touchy. We'll leave those to our ambassador in Nassau, but I'm going to want you on hand to personally brief our chargé d'affaires down there. I want him to know how serious things are . . . and what the repercussions will be if we cannot shut Pirate's Cay down, and fast.

"Also, I'm ordering RAMROD Mobile One readied to fly down there. They'll bring along Rod's Combat Mod."

"If I might suggest," Rod added. "This would be an excellent opportunity to field test the Sea Mod as well. Dr. McDaniels said last week that it was ready for trials."

"I'll talk to her about it."

Drake continued to listen to the planning for the logistical end of the operation, but said nothing. He knew when he was beaten, and he knew both how to take orders . . . and when those orders could be bent. And with technical support, spare parts and repairs would be quickly available if Rod should be damaged in the fight.

He just hoped that Rod survived the reconnaissance in the first place, so that the RAMROD technicians had something left to work on.

⬥Chapter Eight

. . . Carlos Ferré is believed to have gotten his start as a sicario, one of the teenage hit men who serve as assassins-for-hire for the various Colombian drug cartels. At the age of eighteen he was employed by the Ochoa-Escobar cartel and is believed to have organized distribution networks in Washington and Philadelphia.

"Ferré has personally killed at least twenty-seven men, most of them lower-level dealers who could not pay for his deliveries, and he is known to have given the orders for the execution of many others. He is considered intelligent, but unstable, unpredictable, and extremely dangerous. . . .

In his third-floor office at CIA headquarters at Langley, James Weston snapped off the computer monitor and swiveled his leather chair around so that he could stare out the window into the cool Virginia night. The sleek, modern structure was virtually surrounded by woods, and only a tell-tale, hazy glow above the trees to the southeast revealed the presence of Washington, D.C., a few miles away and across the Potomac River.

The Agency records on Carlos Ferré were revealing, but they failed to communicate the true danger of the man.

Ferré, if the hints the CIA was receiving were true, was opening new pipelines, buying local authorities, opening new sources of intelligence. . . .

If drugs were big business in America, Ferré was on his way to becoming the General Motors of cocaine.

The man himself was not as important as what he represented. Carlos Ferré was a mid- to high-level distributor of cocaine, which put him between the people who controlled its sale in American cities and the big-name bosses of the Colombian cartels, the Ochoas, the Escobars, the Salazars, and others. He was one of those responsible for actually smuggling the cartels' deadly white poison into the United States . . . and it was he, and others like him, who were responsible for the wholesale corruption of the police, of military personnel, of the governments of half a dozen countries, from Colombia to the United States herself.

Weston sighed. The enemies were not all in South America, or on remote Bahamian islands.

He'd not told Chris Drake everything. The evening sky outside was clear and star-dusted, but a storm was gathering down the river in Washington, a storm that might well sweep him away, along with RAMROD and everything he'd worked for for the past six years.

Somehow, word had leaked about RAMROD . . . and about an American combat robot that had for the past six months been routinely violating international law by carrying out military operations on foreign soil.

James Weston had been recruited to the CIA in 1953. Starting his intelligence career in the Office of Global Issues, he'd eventually been put in charge of keeping track of the growing tangle of international drug-smuggling networks, especially the cocaine pipelines coming out of Colombia and into the United States.

He'd known, as well as any other man alive, just how

deadly the flood of white poison across America's borders was. And in 1986, he'd been approached by Senator Buchanan to head up Project RAMROD.

The idea of delivering a high-tech combat robot onto foreign soil, of turning it loose against the gangsters and drug lords and mafia dons who were systematically destroying America, was preposterous no matter how you looked at it. How could one machine—however intelligent, fast, or deadly—do what Coast Guard cutters, Navy Hawkeye radar planes, the entire Border Patrol, and battalions of DEA agents had failed to do and stop the deadly, incoming tide of white poison?

And yet, the evidence seemed to suggest that one robot was doing just that. Block the pipelines, and the drug lords found other pipelines . . . usually faster than they could be identified and traced. But go after the drug lords themselves . . .

WHITE SANCTION was the code name for the ongoing program of targeting the drug kingpins where they lived, of going in and capturing or killing them and destroying the labs and warehouses and private fortresses that kept them in power. So far, Cybernarc had shut down half a dozen heroin labs and cocaine factories and had punched the tickets for perhaps ten or twelve major players on the international drug smuggling scene. That represented the proverbial drop in the proverbial bucket, an almost insignificant scratch in the vast and complex network of underworld narcotics trafficking.

But Weston's sources were reporting that WHITE SANCTION was having an effect on that network entirely out of proportion to its size. Once the narcotics traffickers learned that Cybernarc was targeting, not their pipelines, but *them*, it became an intensely personal war.

The drug lords had already begun diverting huge percentages of their profits into self-defense, profits that would otherwise have gone back into their business of stealing souls. Many had shut down operations entirely, and there were

reports of purges within the ranks of several of the more powerful cartels as their leaders became increasingly suspicious
of their own people. One story coming out of Mexico had it
that members of a drug ring had taken to ritually slashing
parts of their bodies with razors to prove that they could
bleed and were, therefore, human. Another from Tokyo
reported that the Yakuza, Japan's home-grown version of the
Mafia, was assuring its clients that its old custom of amputat-
ing finger joints in order to demonstrate loyalty to the clan
chiefs was the best proof there was that that sinister organization had not been penetrated by American CIA robots.

In short, WHITE SANCTION was working. After six months,
Project RAMROD had the drug lords rattled. In another six
months, it might even have them on the run.

But it was beginning to look like RAMROD would not
have another six months . . . or even another six weeks. The
machinery for dismantling the program was already being
moved into place.

The House Intelligence Committee, created in the wake of
the Church hearings of the '70s, was charged with oversight
of all American intelligence activities. In particular, it was
designed to provide a check against the CIA, a way of keeping that organization from returning to the bad old days of
unrestrained—and illegal—operations against foreign governments and leaders. By law, no government agency could
target foreign nationals for assassination; by law, no agency
or individual could conduct military operations against
sovereign nations with which the United States was not at
war. The Neutrality Act had been on the books in one form
or another since 1948, but now Congress seemed determined to enforce it . . . and to interpret it, as well.

And what was worse, in a highly controversial twist of par-
tisan politics the year before, the House Speaker had named
six congressmen to the committee, each of whom had a vest-

ed interest in crippling American intelligence activities. One was self-professed admirer of Castro who had openly supported Grenada's Marxist revolution and tried to initiate impeachment proceedings against Reagan after that island's invasion. The others had routinely served as mouthpieces for the Sandanistas and their Marxist dictatorship in Nicaragua. Several had been responsible for serious leaks to the world press concerning sensitive U.S. intelligence activities, and one had publicly declared that every American intelligence agency should be totally dismantled, "piece by piece, nail by nail, brick by brick."

And it was just possible that WHITE SANCTION had given those men the tools they needed to do the job.

The debate over just what a national intelligence organization ought to be allowed to do dragged on, but in the meantime, the CIA had continued with some projects that were questionable under the current laws. Usually, there were ways to bury these with other "black programs" so that the anti-intelligence community couldn't examine and expose them . . . but this time, something had gone wrong. Two days earlier, a Democratic congressman from California—and one of the members of the Intelligence Committee—had mentioned both RAMROD and WHITE SANCTION openly during a debate on the House floor, using them as examples of "unregulated" CIA intelligence activities.

Whether the security breach was intentional or accidental was unknown; what *was* known was that the leak, televised by C-SPAN and picked up by the evening news of four networks, had ignited a firestorm of debate on Capitol Hill, and the promise of a House investigation into CIA activities in the drug war.

Cybernarc was well on his way to becoming a celebrity, a development that could ruin his effectiveness in the drug wars.

The fact of the matter was, Weston thought, WHITE SANCTION *was* illegal, and, however tenuous the official connections, RAMROD was still carried on the books as a CIA project, funded through the Directorate of Science and Technology. If and when the whole story came out, the CIA would shut down RAMROD overnight. WHITE SANCTION would be canceled and RAMROD would lose its funding, its political support, and its very reason for existence. Never mind that targeting the drug lords was turning out to be the most successful of the dozens of strategies tried to date; the publicity alone would destroy Cybernarc's effectiveness, and the political fallout would kill him.

The results for America at large could be disastrous. How much time was left, he wondered, on the countdown set ticking by the Buchanan Report? Was Senator Buchanan right? Would America herself be destroyed by the festering rot of crime and corruption spread by drugs and drug money? How long before that cancer eating away at America destroyed the very laws and rights that made operations like WHITE SANCTION illegal?

There was more riding on Operation SEA KING than Drake and Rod knew. Weston desperately needed a victory in the drug war. Cocaine labs burned in Colombia, a warlord's fortress destroyed in Burma . . . these were victories, to be sure, but what was necessary now was an indication that RAMROD and WHITE SANCTION were turning the tide against the death merchants who were operating openly within the United States. A major drug bust, say, made possible by intelligence provided by Rod. The arrest of a major trafficker . . . like Carlos Ferré. *Anything* that could convince Capitol Hill and the White House that RAMROD was a useful weapon in this damned, bloody war.

For that reason alone, Weston had authorized Rod's solo probe into the hornets' nest on Pirate's Cay. He accepted the robot's assessment that the chances for success were better if he went in alone; Weston was gambling the entire program on the hope that Rod's intelligence could be used by Group Seven in their political fight for survival.

If Rod succeeded, there was a chance that RAMROD could be salvaged. If he failed, he would almost certainly be destroyed.

But then, if he failed, the robot was almost certainly doomed anyway, dismantled with Project RAMROD. As far as Weston knew, robots had no civil rights, no right to fair trial or hearing . . .

. . . or even a right to life.

Rod searched the darkness, blending infrared input with computer-enhanced LI data. From the cockpit of the runabout he could detect nothing ashore out of the ordinary, no warm bodies, no hot engine blocks, no probing flashlights. The half moon rising in the east shed light enough to distinguish surf from sand and the black shadows of the trees beyond. The beach was deserted.

He was detecting a steady, pulsing thrum at radar wavelengths, which suggested that the motorboat might already have been picked up by the radar on Pirate's Cay. That wouldn't matter, though. So far as the drug runners on the island were concerned, the motorboat was one of hundreds of craft in these waters, out before the dawn for some early-morning fishing.

The robot turned to face the boat's pilot. Drake had cut the engines back to idle and was allowing the runabout to coast gently toward the black mass of the cay.

"Technically," Rod said, "you are violating orders being here."

"Yeah," the SEAL agreed. "But you don't think I was

going to let anyone else run you out here, did you?"

"I suspected that you were going to try to make me change my mind. Or come with me."

Drake made a sour face that he must have thought was hidden in the darkness. Through his LI optics, Rod could see it clearly.

"I may disobey orders from time to time," Drake said. "But mutiny ain't my style."

They chugged through the moonlit sea for several more minutes, before Drake broke the silence. "Hey, Rod? How do you make decisions?"

"I do not understand the question."

"When you're faced with a problem, you don't know what to do . . . how do you make up your mind?"

"At any given time I am simultaneously running several parallel programs governing more or less autonomic reflexes, data acquisition, and biomimicry routines. In addition, my PARET programming provides general guidelines for behavior, especially when dealing with military activities. When faced with the need to make a specific decision, I would acquire and assess all available data. Generally it is possible to ascertain a numerical value, expressed as a percentage, which suggests the proper course of action."

"Percentages. Suppose it's fifty-fifty?"

"That would be an unlikely—"

"Suppose you come up against a situation you haven't been exposed to before."

"Such as what?"

"Oh, I don't know. Some quirk of human behavior, something you don't understand. Maybe it's a situation where numbers don't help, a crisis where you'd have to rely on gut instinct."

"I cannot rely on what you refer to as 'gut instinct.' "

"Nope. That's my point. You don't have instincts, and

your guts are silicon chips and plastic circuit boards. So if you had to make a snap judgment without enough data to go on, what would you do?"

"I would rely on the judgment of humans. That, after all, was why they assigned you as my partner."

Drake nodded slowly. "Yeah. But tonight you're going in there on your own. Watch yourself, huh?"

They were silent for several minutes. Rod seemed thoughtful. "We have discussed the phenomenon referred to as 'combat instincts' before. There have been times when I have acted on data which my programming assessed as incomplete. The episode in Nassau when I set up an ambush without consulting you was one instance. Another was when I came to your aid at the marina. I find that I cannot always . . . explain my actions."

Drake looked at him sharply. "You surprise me. Does that mean you have feelings?"

Rod did not answer immediately. The rumble of the boat's engine was barely audible above the slap of water on the hull.

"I have responses deliberately incorporated into my basic programming which might be interpreted as feelings," he said slowly. "A sense of satisfaction for a successfully completed task. An impulse to preserve myself in the face of danger which could be termed fear or caution. Why do you ask?"

"I just wondered. Sometimes I wonder just how human you really are."

Rod thought about this for a long time. He did not want to reveal the turmoil of—there was no other word—*emotions*, that inward chaos he'd felt since sharing a PARET link with Drake the night the SEAL's family had been killed. At first, the inner churnings could be dismissed . . . or ignored.

But they were becoming stronger. More intense.

And he didn't know if they were good or bad. Some of them—feelings of loyalty and camaraderie and dedication to the mission—he thought were good.

But the hatred, the burning hatred of the drug lords and what they were doing, what they had done . . .

Was hatred good? A lust for vengeance . . . a wrenching, burning desire to hunt down the drug lords on their home grounds and crush the life from their bodies . . . was that good? Or that devastating, all-encompassing loneliness that rose sometimes like a black specter in the back of his mind . . . what was that?

But to admit such human feelings was to admit that something was wrong with him.

And, in a most human-like refusal to face an unpleasant truth, Rod did not want to make that admission, not yet.

Not if it meant losing them when the RAMROD project technicians began dumping memory in an effort to discover what was wrong. In a strange way, Rod was coming to accept those emotions as a part of who and what he was.

He wasn't ready to lose that part of himself, not when he still didn't know what those feelings were . . . or who he was.

"Sometimes," Rod said at last, "I wonder about that myself. Speculation, however, would be fruitless. I am a machine, designed and built to carry out my specific programming."

"Yeah, like you did when you rewrote your own programming so you didn't have to obey an order. Right."

Rod did not want to discuss the question further. "This is close enough. I must check my equipment."

With Commander Baird's authorization, he'd equipped himself for the mission at AUTEC's supply depot. His slacks, sweatshirt, Kevlar vest and combat harness, leather gloves, and sneakers were all black, as was the wool balaclava that covered his entire face except for his eyes. A human, he reflected, would have felt uncomfortably hot wearing such garments in the subtropics, but here the robot's lack of sweat glands and his internal temperature control would be an advantage. Used to changing his body almost at will, he did not feel the discomfort of wet, hot, or scratchy clothing.

He carried a black canvas pouch, like a backpack with a carrying strap. Inside was an Uzi submachine gun equipped with a sound suppressor, five extra 32-round magazines, and six grenades. Also in the pack, sealed in waterproof plastic, was an AN/PRC-620 and a battery pack. The powerful little radio would give him over-the-horizon voice communication with AUTEC, his lifeline to Drake and the other humans backing up his mission.

Strapped in its outsized holster on his right leg was a SEAL special, a silenced, 9mm Smith & Wesson Mark 22 Model O automatic, the infamous Hush Puppy, the sound-suppressed pistol favored by Navy commando teams since Vietnam.

Rod hoped to avoid combat on the island, but if avoidance was impossible, he was going to face it prepared.

He felt Drake's hand rest briefly on his shoulder. "You remember what I said. Watch yourself in there, okay?"

"I will be careful."

"I'll be waiting to hear from you. Don't lose that radio."

"Affirmative." Rod grasped the canvas bag tight against his side, seated himself on the runabout's port gunnel, then rolled backward into the sea.

The bottom here was sandy and firmly packed, the water less than four meters deep. Rod landed on his feet, then ran a quick systems check.

Functional and operational . . . with no leaks and no malfunctions. Excellent. He waited as the muted thunder of the runabout's engine gathered power, then faded. Orienting himself by his inner compass, he started walking toward the west.

Progress was slow, his movements underwater necessarily slow-paced and tedious. The water was completely black, opaque at both visible and IR wavelengths.

He had a machine's patience, however, and did not feel exhaustion the way a human would. Ten minutes after entering the water, he began to sense the back-and-forth surge of the waves above him, and the swift tug of undertow around his legs. The sea floor rose sharply, and then the surf was breaking around his head and shoulders. As his eyes came clear of the water, he quickly scanned the beach and forest, now only twenty meters ahead. In the brief interlude before the next wave submerged his head once more, he was able to verify that the beach was still deserted.

Five minutes later, Rod rose from the sea like a black, high-tech Aphrodite, water cascading from his sides and back and foaming around his sneakers. That classical illusion, he realized, was not quite right. Rod had come to Pirate's Cay not as the sea-borne goddess of love, but as a black-clad god of death.

He stepped onto the beach, conscious that each step left a deep, water-filled print in the sand. The tide was coming in, however. Within an hour his tracks should have been erased from the shore.

And by that time he would be well inland. He paused for a few minutes by the treeline, checking weapons, ammo, and the all-important radio.

All correct. His internal clock registered 0235 hours. He oriented himself on both the Pirate's Cay airfield and the hilltop villa, then started off.

Operation SEA KING had begun.

⬤ᴡ Chapter Nine

HE WAS A SHADOW AMONG SHADOWS, slipping across the villa's defensive perimeter as silently as a cat. He'd stashed the radio in the woods half a kilometer from the villa and carried only the Uzi with him.

To Rod's LI- and IR-sensitive optics, the area was illuminated day bright. On the ground, soft-glowing patches of color marked where men had walked minutes earlier, and he could see the heat smears of every guard, hot vehicle engine, and burning cigarette tip within a kilometer. His audio receptors picked up conversations at a range of 200 meters, while his internal processors separated words from background hash, allowing him to listen in on Ferré's troops as they talked in low voices over a shared bottle or marijuana joint. Avoiding them was like a high-tech round of blind man's bluff played in reverse; Rod could see perfectly while everyone else in the game could not.

His first stop was the airstrip north of the villa. A De Havilland cargo plane was parked on the runway, its twin turboprop nacelles glowing white hot to Rod's IR vision. A number of men were unloading what looked like aluminum canisters out of the plane and stacking them aboard a pair of utility trucks parked on the tarmac. Rod had not heard the plane and guessed it had landed while he and Drake were still some distance out at sea. The unloading was nearly complete.

Next he swung south toward the villa.

In the days when Vista del Mar had been a vacation resort, the Strand had been the name of the resort's guest accommodations. Located at the eastern foot of the hill, it looked like a small motel set back in the woods, an angled row of modern-looking apartments, two stories high, with tennis courts, a swimming pool, and a short path through the trees to a secluded white beach. There was a fence up around the building now, with a single gate. From the forest Rod could see two sentries at the gate, with others patrolling the railed balcony of the second-floor apartments.

Despite telescopic vision and computer enhancement, he could not see through the windows, for the drapes were drawn on every one. Once, though, four of Ferré's men walked past the guards at the front gate with boisterous shouts and an exchange of bantering, joking insults. They'd used a key to enter one of the first-floor apartments, and seconds later Rod could hear faint, shrill screams, women's screams, blending with a baby's crying.

Rod remembered Drake's comment about women and children in Windsor. The Strand, apparently, was where at least some of the women and children were being held, hostages to control the rest of the people in town . . . and evidently a source of entertainment for the invaders as well.

Three hundred meters further up the slope from the Strand, beyond the tennis court and pool, the villa of Vista del Mar rose from the hilltop, a modernistic sprawl of redwood, glass, and tile. The exterior was brilliantly lit by floodlights, and more guards paced their rounds within pools of harsh light. In some ways, they were easier to avoid than the men in the woods. Rod located one of the ground lights set into its socket in the ground and deftly unscrewed the bulb just enough to darken it. That left one part of the open ground around the former resort only partly lit, and Rod made his way through the shadows and up to the building wall. The guards, their night vision ruined by the batteries of floodlights, saw nothing.

Rod wanted to see the inside of the villa. How strongly was it reinforced? Were there heavy weapons mounted at the windows? Were the hallways and inner rooms heavily guarded?

And where was Carlos Ferré? It was possible that the drug lord lived in some other house on the island, a less conspicuous place that would give him ready escape routes off the island in case of a surprise attack.

At least, that was what Rod would have done in Ferré's place. Putting himself in the enemy's place was basic to much of the small-unit tactics he'd PARETed from Drake and other combat specialists. In this instance, though, it was possible that the enemy felt secure enough not to bother with elaborate precautions. Vista del Mar was by far the most luxurious residence on Pirate's Cay, and with its secluded location at the crest of the island's highest hill, it was probably the most defensible.

What would he do if he encountered Ferré now? The robot considered the possibility with the dispassionate objectivity possible only to a computer. He was here to gather intelligence only, with a view to returning in force later. But suppose he bumped into Ferré within the next few moments . . . what then?

He remembered Drake's probing questions earlier in the boat. Suppose he had to make the decision, and there was no clear way to juggle the numbers. He would have to make a decision for which humans would use instinct, a gut decision . . . and Rod was simply not equipped for that kind of confrontation.

Encountering Ferré in person would be such a situation.

Killing Ferré would complete the WHITE SANCTION op against the man . . . but the current mission called for stealth, for sneaking in, gathering information, and escaping once more without leaving any traces of his presence.

After considering the question for several milliseconds, Rod elected a totally human solution to the problem. He would continue the mission—*Charlie Mike*, as his human counterparts would say—and worry about killing Ferré only if he actually ran into the guy.

Meanwhile, he had to find a way to carry his probe into the villa.

From a hiding place behind a low, ornamental wall, he watched as a pickup truck arrived, rolling up to the front door of the house and parking in the drive. Eight soldiers piled out. They were unarmed but wearing the mismatched uniforms of the guards and sentries he'd encountered so far.

One of them seemed to be in charge. "Inside," he said in Spanish. "Downstairs." He pointed to three armed men who'd been standing guard outside the front of the villa. "You three go, too. Dr. Max needs help moving some equipment. You go, too!"

Rod sensed solitary footsteps at his back.

One of the sentries came around the corner of the house, a young man about Rod's height, wearing jungle camouflage fatigues and a black beret, with an AK-47 slung barrel down at his back. Rod sprang from the shadows, closing on the guard from behind. His right hand swept over the man's face, snapping back, as his left fist smashed into the soldier's spine. There was a single, sharp crack. Rod lowered the body silently to the ground, then dragged it to the cover of some flowering bougainvillea nearby.

Moments later, Rod reappeared, wearing the uniform and beret. His own combat blacks, the silenced Uzi, his Hush Puppy and knife were all hidden with the body of the guard.

Sauntering casually around to the front of the house, he approached the two sentries standing on the villa's front porch.

"Hola, compadres!" he called. "They said Dr. Max is looking for men to move some equipment."

"Inside," one of the guards said. "Down the stairs and to your right."

"Mil gracias."

His penetration of the enemy fortress was that easy.

Inside, he wandered through luxuriously furnished and carpeted hallways, but his eye—backed by computer enhancement and a literally photographic memory for details—took in more sinister aspects of the villa's architecture.

Surveillance cameras were mounted in various corners, scanning each hallway, and he could hear the low-frequency hum of electronic warning systems at most doors. In places, he could see where walls had been reinforced, and steel shutters had been installed at strategic points where they could slam shut during an emergency. Peering through one open door into what had once been a dining room, he saw two men manning a Russian-made PKM machine gun at a window that overlooked the villa's front lawn.

The place was a fortress. If it was attacked, every approach would be covered by machine-gun fire. Any direct assault would take heavy casualties.

He heard someone coming, but since he was in the field of view of a security camera, he appeared to take no notice.

"What are you doing in here?"

"Excuse me, señor," Rod said, removing his beret. "They told me Dr. Max needed men to move some equipment and sent me here. I guess I got lost."

The man, grim-faced and competent-looking, eyed Rod up and down. "Very well. Follow me."

"Thank you, señor. It is a confusing place."

His guide said nothing but ushered him down a set of

wooden steps to a stone-floored basement. A heavy wooden door opened into a stone room that might once have been a storage room or wine cellar.

Inside was chaos. Several soldiers were already there, moving a heavy chest out through the door as soon as Rod entered. Two more worked at the room's only other door, which appeared to open to the outside and a flight of stone steps going up. They seemed to be removing part of the door with a saw, high up near the top.

In one corner, a white-haired man in a leather apron was attending to an injured man.

No . . . a prisoner. Despite the mangled features, Rod recognized Benny Armitage. He'd been stretched out on a table top, tied at wrists and ankles, with his torso and legs covered by a sheet. A bottle hung upside-down from a pole above his head. The white-haired man was sliding the IV needle into a vein at the hollow of Armitage's elbow.

"Dr. Vargas?" the man who'd brought Rod down said.

The doctor taped the needle in place. "What is it, Sergeant Muñoz?" he said, not looking up. With the needle secure, he adjusted the IV's rate of flow.

Muñoz gestured toward Rod. "Another pair of hands. Where do you want him?"

Vargas looked around briefly and with impatience. "Have him stand by. It is crowded enough in here as it is."

Muñoz pointed to the back wall of the room and indicated that Rod should stand there, out of the way. The soldiers appeared to be clearing the room completely, carrying out boxes and crates.

Standing silently at parade rest, Rod reviewed the information gathered to date. He'd counted seventy-two soldiers so far, both within and outside the villa. Dr. Vargas was the first civilian he'd seen, but there would be others. With the possible exception of Sergeant Muñoz, the soldiers he'd encountered so far were poorly trained and indifferently equipped. It was their numbers that made them formidable . . . their numbers and the presence of an unknown number of machine guns mounted at strategic points throughout the house.

The activity in the basement was puzzling. Was Ferré preparing to withdraw from the villa? Or was he simply removing evidence of the uses to which this wine cellar had been put? So far, there was not enough data for Rod to make a determination.

He turned his head unobtrusively to study Armitage and was surprised to see the prisoner staring back at him with an intense, knowing gaze.

Armitage had recognized him.

Rod allowed no expression to touch his features. He tried to read Armitage's expression without success. The enlargement of his pupils suggested that he'd received a massive dose of some painkiller, probably so that he could be moved without killing him. That suggested they intended to keep him alive, though it was obvious that they'd been working him over pretty hard. His mouth gaped open, leaking drool. An indistinct sound rasped past cracked, swollen lips.

Automatically, Rod recorded the sound, analyzed it, enhanced it. Two syllables . . . probably two words and probably English rather than Spanish, but garbled and slurred. He enhanced them again, playing them back silently within his memory.

"Kill . . . me. . . ."

Rod remained impassive. Armitage continued to stare at him, silently pleading.

Muñoz reappeared at the doorway. "Dr. Vargas? Where do you want the prisoner?"

"Upstairs," the doctor replied. "One of the free bedrooms in the north wing. Wait a moment. We'll need to set up an IV pole next to the bed. . . ."

He hurried out the door.

Only two soldiers remained in the room, the men who were still sawing a hole in the outside door. Neither was paying any attention to Rod, or to the sheet-draped man on the table.

He moved to Armitage's side, the prisoner's eyes following his movements. The man spoke again, the words almost drowned in the hiss-shriek of the saw.

"Please . . . kill me. . . ."

How badly was Armitage hurt? The injuries to his face were superficial, cuts and bruises, a broken nose. He'd been beaten, but not too badly. Deftly, Rod lifted the sheet . . .

. . . and understood. The burns were savage, raw, and oozing. There were branded spots where hot irons had left their mark; in places, on chest, stomach, and the ruined horror of his genitals, some flammable liquid had been poured, then ignited.

Rod had only an academic understanding of pain. Sensors within the plastic sheathing that imitated human skin served to warn him of impact, of heat, or cold. Pain was one of those human traits that he could comprehend, but never experience. First-aid training PARETed from those who knew described serious burns as among the most painful of wounds. Even when nerve endings were totally destroyed by charring, the surrounding tissue would be shrieking circles of agony. Armitage must be either deeply in shock or heavily sedated now to endure such damage silently.

Or possibly, Rod reflected, the human mechanism could only be pushed so far before it overloaded and burned out, just like any electrically powered machine.

"Kill . . ."

Rod dropped the sheet, glancing again at the workers across the room. They had completed sawing a square hole in the door and were inspecting their work.

Swiftly, Rod grasped Armitage's head between his hands, lifted it slightly, then wrenched suddenly and sharply to the left. The prisoner's final breath escaped in a long, ragged hiss through parted lips.

With two flicks of his powerful forefinger, Rod parted the bonds around Armitage's wrists. With the soldiers' backs turned, he pulled the body into a seated position, then gave it a hard push to the side as he sprang lightly back toward his original position next to the wall.

The corpse toppled over the side of the table. There was a resounding crash as the IV stand clattered to the floor and the glass bottle exploded in shards and splattering liquid. The soldiers at the door spun, startled by the noise.

"El prisionero!" Rod shouted. "He's trying to escape!"

The soldiers were across the room in a second, examining the naked body, which hung halfway off the table, still secured by its ankles and entangled in the sheet. "He's not going to get very far," one of them said, lifting the head off the stone floor, then letting it fall. "He broke his neck."

"Stay here," Rod said. He hurried out the door. "I'll get Dr. Vargas."

As he made his way up the steps, he wondered at his own motivation. Why had he killed Armitage? There was no programmed imperative to put torture victims out of their misery . . . and if one of those soldiers had turned at the wrong moment, Rod would have had to kill all of them. That would have alerted Ferré and seriously compromised the mission.

There was, however, somewhere deep within him, a feeling of responsibility . . . and of regret, of a debt unpaid. He could not put it into words, but Rod knew that it had been his decision to leave Armitage tied up aboard the *Junebug* at Hurricane Hole, his fault that the man had been captured.

Killing Armitage had been the only way Rod could think of that could even begin to even the score. It was, after all, what Armitage himself had wanted.

Rod hoped that his decision had been the right one.

* * *

The sun was rising, illuminating Windsor Bay in copper
and gold. A black Chrysler drove into town from the north,
swinging past the vacant church and onto Waterfront Drive.
It was followed by an olive drab pickup and two canvas-cov-
ered trucks.

The locals were already waiting when the convoy pulled
up, sullen and resentful as always, but Ferré didn't care. He
needed them now, because some were known in Nassau, and
their disappearance would raise questions in the Bahamian
capital, but soon he'd be able to dispense with them entirely.

They would not make the mistakes Lehder had made at
Norman's Cay. Soon, the final arrangements would be made
in Nassau, the last officials reached and paid off, and then
they could import a Colombian work force, men and women
willing to work enthusiastically for Ferré in exchange for the
promise of a new life.

The rest of the locals, well . . . they'd lived such secluded
lives out here on the fringes of the islands, few people even
knew they were here. They could be made to vanish without
much fuss.

He got out of the car. Estrada walked up from the direction of the seaplane hangar. "Everything is ready to go,
Carlos."

"Excellent. Let's get it moving."

Happily, he watched his men herd the sullen townspeople
onto the dock.

Ten meters away, at Ferré's back, a shadow detached itself
from the bottom of the pickup, then slid across the pavement
in a flowing surge, black on asphalt black. Rod had discard-

ed the borrowed uniform for his combat blacks once more, and the sound-suppressed Uzi was strapped across his back. No one saw him slip silently into the cover of oil drums and fishing nets draped across drying racks near the dock.

There was a terrible temptation to execute the WHITE SANCTION portion of his mission here and now. A touch on the trigger of his Uzi, and Ferré would be dead.

There'd been far too many armed men about at the villa for him to take a shot, and the situation was even worse here at the dock. He would never be able to handle them all, and it was imperative that he report to Weston and Drake what he saw resting on the seaplane ramp.

It looked like a raft, twelve meters long and six wide, made of aluminum spars linking flotation tanks, and covered over by planks and canvas straps. There were also wings, stubby, down-canted affairs that seemed designed to provide lift. At the bow, a harness attachment was linked to a massive cable.

At gunpoint, the locals were unloading metal canisters from the trucks and handing them down to six of Ferré's men working on the raft. Each container was a meter long and twice the thickness of a man's thigh, and weighed, Rod estimated, twenty kilos. He counted 250 of the canisters as they were secured to the raft in a pile five wide, ten long, and five high, strapped side by side and one atop another until it looked like the raft could not possibly hold even one more.

Five tons . . .

The cargo had to be cocaine. The cable suggested that they planned to tow the raft, and the flotation tanks meant they could submerge it behind the tow boat. That was how they planned to smuggle the shipment ashore unseen.

But what was the destination? The landing point could be anywhere at all in the thousand kilometers of coast from Key West to Savannah.

Rod could think of only one way to find out.

✒ Chapter Ten

ROD SPENT MUCH of the rest of that day exploring Pirate's Cay. Once the cargo loading was complete, the raft was covered by a tarpaulin and left under guard.

He doubted that the shipment would remain for long on the seaplane ramp. The best time to move it would be after dark. From the air, the crystal shallows around the Bahamas were transparent, and a boat towing an underwater raft would be instantly spotted, and its cargo recognized for what it was.

He would return to the dock at nightfall.

In the meantime, Rod mapped the island almost meter by meter, locating clear fields of fire, defensive positions, and clearings that could serve as landing zones. He returned to the villa at midday, setting up an OP from which he could watch the house and its approaches.

At one point, he moved down the hill and attempted to probe the security around the Strand but was unable to get close enough to learn if Congressman Rutherford was being held in any of the apartments. There were prisoners in those locked and guarded rooms, certainly. At noon he saw guards delivering paper bags, probably meals, but whether any of the rooms held other than captive islanders, he couldn't tell.

He spent most of the afternoon at his OP, recording the movements and schedules of guards, and watching for another opportunity to hit Carlos Ferré.

That there were advantages to being human Rod was more than willing to admit. But there were advantages to being a robot as well.

One of the largest of them was that he could be very, very patient.

Ferré mounted the stairs leading to the second floor of the villa. The faint sound of sawing floated up to the first floor from the basement, followed by the bang-bang-bang of a hammer.

"Señor Ferré?"

"What is it, Muñoz?"

"The men are dispersed, as you ordered. Everything is ready."

"Bueno."

"There's just one thing. We have another man missing."

"Another! You're sure?"

"Yes, sir. A guard outside the house. He did not report at morning muster."

Ferré scowled. That made five of his men gone in the past twenty-four hours, vanished without a trace. It was possible they had taken a small boat and left the island . . . but unlikely. They all knew what would happen if they were caught.

"Send some trusted people into Nassau," he told Muñoz. "Maybe they decided to visit the casino or something."

"Yes, sir." Muñoz did not sound convinced.

"You think there's a problem?"

"I don't know, *Jefé*. I just keep remembering how fast, how quietly *el Cybernarco* moved. . . ."

"The Cybernarc. Yes."

"Four men on patrol, vanished . . . and no indication that a boat was missing. And now, one of our guards . . ."

"You think it could be the robot?"

"It is possible."

"So much the better. I was afraid he might not come."

"This . . . this *thing* is very dangerous. You don't know—"

"I know, Sergeant, that I am relying on you to provide security for this operation. Do your job well, and you will be the richest man in all of Cuba, richer even than Fidel. Fail me . . ."

He turned away and continued up the stairs.

Cybernarc. The death of Benny Armitage had been nagging at him since the discovery of the body early that morning. How could the prisoner have managed to break those ropes with his body as burned, torn, and drugged as it was? There was no evidence to suggest that the accident was anything other than what it seemed, and yet . . .

He hoped it *was* Cybernarc. All of his defensive preparations were built on that hope . . . and on the picture of the robot he was piecing together from various sources.

Know your enemy. That rule had guided him out of the hell of the Medellín streets, had brought him wealth and power, had put him on top of the pack. So far, the enemy had, for the most part, been the sharks of the Colombian drug world, cunning, but predictable in their own way.

This enemy would be no different. He was determined to defeat it in the same way.

Upstairs, he let one of his men unlock the door and precede him into the room, then stepped through the door himself, imperious, hands on hips. The prisoner sat slumped on the bed, hands clasped before him, head down.

"Good afternoon, Mr. Congressman," Ferré said. "I promised that we'd have a little chat, after you'd had a chance to rest, to think things over."

Rutherford's head came up, his eyes filled with a cold fury. "You bastard. Where is she?"

"Now, Clyde. You seem so negative! Is that any kind of attitude to take?"

"Where is my wife?"

"Quite safe, Mr. Congressman. For now."

"Let me see her. Take me to her!"

"Well, that wasn't part of our agreement, was it? I still have questions to ask of you, questions about Group Seven."

"But I don't know anything about it."

"You *will* do what I ask, Clyde. After you tell me about Group Seven, I may even let you return to Washington, but . . ." He held up his forefinger, wagging it slowly back and forth for emphasis. "But, June will stay here. For the time being, at least. As our . . . guest."

"I'm not going anywhere without her, you filthy—"

"Really, Clyde, how did you get to be a successful politician with such a confrontational attitude? The choice is simple. Either you do what I tell you, or your beautiful wife gets the same gentle loving we gave your friend Betty. Naked, strapped to a table, with my boys taking turns while you sit by and watch. You know, some of my people, they are already making bets on whether June will last longer than Betty did. What do you think?"

"No! No, please—"

"Do we understand each other?"

"Yes . . ." Rutherford's voice cracked. He swallowed. "Yes."

"All right, then. You can start by telling me if you've ever heard of something called *Cybernarc.* . . ."

The drug lord never showed himself. After watching the

villa for five hours, sixteen minutes, Rod uncoiled himself from the position where he'd been waiting.

The activity around the villa was puzzling, and he would have liked to investigate it further, especially considering the fact that it was probably related to the defense of the building. While he'd been watching, two cement-mixer trucks had arrived from the direction of town. They'd backed up behind the house right next to the steps that led down to the basement room where he'd found and killed Benny Armitage.

But, except for the silent pacing of the guards, there was no other activity at all visible at the house.

Finally convinced that Ferré was not going to show himself for an easy kill, Rod backtracked through the woods to the spot where he'd stashed the radio, established contact with AUTEC, and transmitted a brief update of the situation and his request for backup. Without waiting for a reply, he wrapped up the radio again in the plastic waterproofing and secured it inside its carrying pouch.

At sunset, Rod was back in Windsor, still unobserved as far as he could tell. The *Jolly Roger* had been powered up and was idling a few meters off the dock, her stern toward the seaplane ramp, with four armed men aboard. The towing cable had been passed to the boat and secured to a bit on the fantail. At the orders of gun-wielding guards, several of the townspeople slid the heavy raft down the ramp and into the water, where some of Ferré's men appeared to be adjusting the buoyancy of the flotation tanks. Properly trimmed, the raft would remain submerged at a set depth, trailing the *Jolly Roger* in her wake.

Rod watched carefully, waiting for his chance. It came when Carlos Ferré arrived on the docks once more. All eyes were on the drug lord as Rod, clad head to toe in black, satchel and Uzi carefully strapped tight across his back, slipped into the water in the shadow of one of the wooden piers and let himself sink into the inky water.

Carefully, he walked along the bottom, testing each step along the way. He could hear the *Jolly Roger*'s engine idling close by, a low-pitched thrum in the water. He found the base of the seaplane ramp easily enough. The concrete underfoot felt different from the softer mix of sand, mud, and debris—cans, bottles, even tires—tossed in the bay over the years. He did not approach the raft too closely. Even in the fading light the water remained transparent. Instead, he found the cable halfway between the raft and the *Jolly Roger*, grabbed hold, and waited.

Ten minutes later, the *Jolly Roger*'s engines gunned to a harsh roar, the cable tautened beneath Rod's grasp, and he felt himself lifted from the bottom and dragged forward through the water.

The only way to learn where Ferré's shipment was going was to follow it. As the boat picked up speed at the harbor mouth, Rod eased himself backward, hand over hand, until he reached the raft. There he was able to grab the cross struts and anchor himself firmly in place.

It was going to be a long ride.

Drake looked at Commander Baird with growing horror. "Sir . . . was this *all?*"

"That's it, Lieutenant," the naval officer said, creaking back in his leather chair. They were in Baird's office behind the AUTEC communications center, a small room crammed with books and the high-tech clutter of an IBM PC on his desk.

"God. I leave him alone for a day and what happens?"

He looked again at the message printout, received at the AUTEC communications center while he had been back in Nassau, briefing the U.S. chargé d'affaires at the embassy. It contained a succinct breakdown of paramilitary forces on Pirate's Cay, estimating their total strength at between 125 and 150 men; a verbal description of the villa and its defenses; a description of the Strand complex, and Rod's belief that hostages—including, possibly, Rutherford and his people—were being held there.

" 'Estimated five tons of cocaine are being smuggled into CONUS via sea sled tonight,' " the message continued. Five tons! " 'Am arranging to follow the shipment and will report on its arrival. Coordinate with authorities and have SWAT forces standing by.' " Drake looked up. CONUS—military terminology for the Continental United States—was a hell of a big place. "What the hell does he think he's doing?"

Baird sighed and laid one hand atop the monitor of the desktop computer parked on his desk. "You know, Lieutenant, they started making these things smarter than people, and now they're starting to run things for them-selves. You take Bertha, here. Nothing but trouble since the day they installed her."

"She doesn't work?"

"Oh, she works fine. It's just us humans don't always know what to do with what she tells us."

"Right. Look, Commander, I'm going to need a secure line to Langley again."

"We already passed the word on," Baird said. "As per instructions from your Mr. Weston."

"Fine. I'll need that line anyway. I want to have a few words with my Mr. Weston, ASAP."

It had been a mistake turning Rod loose alone on Pirate's Cay. It wasn't just the fact that two-billion-dollars worth of high-tech hardware was prowling around loose out there. Rod and Drake had been through some tight spots together. Damn it, the robot was his *friend*!

He watched with growing frustration as Baird punched in

the computer code that would open a scrambled satellite link to CIA headquarters.

Rod sensed the flow of the water around him, like a stiff wind but denser. He could see nothing, even with infrared; the water absorbed IR wavelengths too efficiently. But his inner time sense told him they had been underway for three hours, fourteen minutes; his inner compass registered a heading of two-eight-oh; and the force of the water gave him a rough estimate of speed, perhaps fifteen to twenty knots.

That information allowed him to plot an approximate position on a chart projected across his vision field: approximately one hundred miles out from Pirate's Cay, halfway into the Florida Straits.

The waters of the Great Bahamas Banks were quite shallow east of Bimini, in places less than twelve feet deep. But according to his chart, the bottom of the Florida Straits was over five hundred fathoms deep in spots . . . over half a mile straight down. The pressure at that depth would exceed ninety atmospheres, almost fifteen hundred pounds of pressure on every square inch of his body.

If something were to go wrong here, if he were to lose his grip and tumble into the black void below, he knew he would not survive the descent. His hydraulics would not function under such terrific pressures. His inner seals would burst and high-pressure sea water would short out every circuit board, every RAM pack, every piece of electronics in his frame.

Rod clung to the raft's framework and contemplated his own death.

Humans, Rod had concluded, did not think about death often. At least, they rarely discussed it, and the sensations received through PARET sessions seemed to avoid the question. Rod thought of death as cessation. He experienced something of the sort each time they shut him down back at the Farm for servicing or repairs, and there was a deathlike gap, a kind of black emptiness when they shifted his computer core and sensor cluster from one body to another. Once before, on another mission, he'd been hammered to scrap by rocket grenades, and he'd felt life—or what he thought of as life—ebbing from him as short-circuiting wiring drained his power packs. He'd thought then that he was dying.

But to fall here, into these depths, that would be a final death, with no chance for resurrection. Even if he could survive the plunge, the intense pressures, the saltwater intrusion into his electronics, his power source would never last long enough for him to walk out of that chasm.

That would be death, ultimate and complete.

His grip on the sea sled and its deadly cargo tightened.

Half an hour later, he sensed a slowing of the sea sled and a change in direction. According to his compass, they were now heading more or less south, presumably along the Florida coast. What was their destination? A straight line on the original course would have taken them into Hollywood or Fort Lauderdale. South might mean Miami . . . or the cypress swamps south of the city. Wherever Ferré's men were planning on delivering the cocaine, it would have to combine the attributes of remoteness, so that it could be unloaded in privacy, and convenience to the city, for ease of transport.

His radioed message to AUTEC had included a request for a SWAT backup. There were at least four men aboard the *Jolly Roger*, all well armed, and there would be more men—possibly many more—waiting to unload the sled. Five tons was a lot of cargo, and it would take a lot of muscle to unload it. Once he learned where the rendezvous site was, how long would it take to get reinforcements in?

Another hour passed, and he sensed the boat slowing once

more. He could feel a throbbing vibration in the water, the *thrum-thrum-thrum* of a large engine, approaching rapidly.

He still couldn't see. What was happening on the surface?

The *Jolly Roger*'s engine changed sharply in pitch, then died away. The thrumming sound was closer now, coming up rapidly from astern. The heavily laden raft wallowed as it continued to drift forward. The tow line had gone slack. . . .

In a very real way, the sled operated like an aircraft, using its stubby "wings" to fly through the water at a preset depth. Now that it had lost speed, however, it began to angle nose down toward the inky depths.

It took Rod several moments to confirm his first impression. He was sinking, dropping away from the surface rapidly and plunging into the depths. The tow cable was trailing behind the raft now. The *Jolly Roger*'s crew had cast off the line when they'd cut the engines.

Almost certainly, the robot decided, another vessel— probably a Coast Guard cutter—had closed on the *Roger* and ordered her to heave to.

And the *Jolly Roger*'s crew had cast off the tow, sending the raft, its cargo and Rod all plunging into the blackness below.

⦿ Chapter Eleven

COMPUTERS ARE INCAPABLE OF PANIC . . . but the surge and flow of thoughts, perceptions, and commands within Rod's systems might have been mistaken for panic by any observer able to read them. He was sinking, *sinking*, with no way to propel the raft or make himself float.

Plans flashed through his consciousness, each examined, then discarded, in microseconds. If he could propel the raft by kicking his legs . . . negative. The raft was far too massive to respond to the relatively feeble thrust he'd be able to produce. Perhaps the containers with their lethal cargos would float . . . negative. He would need the small amount of air trapped in hundreds of the cylinders to lift his weight, and he had neither time nor means to capture the air. What about the raft's flotation tanks? Each was more than half full of water, but there would be air enough . . . negative. As with the smaller cylinders, he had no way of collecting enough air fast enough.

He was still going down. Of all possible options, attempting to use the flotation tanks seemed the most likely to give him a chance. He would have to make his way to the bottom side of the platform without overturning the raft, then tear the tanks free one by one without rupturing them and . . .

The raft plowed into the bottom with a thump. The shock surprised Rod enormously. He'd begun calculating the raft's rate of descent as soon as it had been cast off by the *Jolly Roger*. If his computations had been accurate, he was resting on the bottom no more than fifteen meters beneath the surface.

It took what for a computer was an eternity—nearly a full second—for Rod to order his mental processes once more. He would not have described his feelings as relief, exactly, but the sudden reassessment of his position made him pause, recycle the rapid-fire flurry of commands flowing through his system, to compose himself until he could think clearly once more. He ran a full systems check.

He was not going to die, after all . . . at least, not yet.

Commander Vincent K. Thomas, U.S. Coast Guard, held the microphone to his lips. "Ahoy, *Jolly Roger*," he said, his amplified voice booming out across the water from the ship's loudhailer. "What is your business?"

Two men appeared on the aft deck of the cabin cruiser, their faces pasty in the searchlight beam. They were wearing bright orange wet suits. One of them cupped his hands to his mouth and called back across the water. "Diving!" he yelled.

The USCGC *Mohawk* was wallowing heavily in the freshening seas. Thomas raised the microphone again but stopped when his communications officer returned. "Skipper? Radio transmission from the target vessel."

"Put it on the speaker."

"Aye, sir."

"Coast Guard Nine-One-Three," a voice said over the radio, reading *Mohawk*'s hull number. "This is Nan-Sierra-Tango-One-Niner-One-Seven, charter boat *Jolly Roger* out of Miami Beach. Do you read me, over?"

"*Jolly Roger*, this is the Coast Guard Cutter *Mohawk*. We read you, over."

"What can we do for you boys, over?"

"*Jolly Roger*, what is your business in these waters, over?"

"Ah, *Mohawk*, we're a charter boat service. Sea View Enterprises, registered in Miami Beach. My clients pay me to take them out scuba diving. My passengers were doing some diving in the Great Banks. We're on our way back to port now. Is there a problem, over?

Thomas studied the cabin cruiser with a hard and practiced eye as she rose and fell under the glare of *Mohawk*'s searchlight. She was not riding low in the water—a dead giveaway for the small craft coming in from Colombia or the Bahamas heavy-laden with marijuana. Her course, as tracked over the past hour on radar, confirmed the story that she'd come across the Florida Straits from the northern Banks, probably somewhere near Bimini. The pilot had immediately obeyed Thomas's order to heave to and had given no reason to suspect that his vessel was carrying anything but what he claimed—scuba divers enjoying some diving off the Great Bahamas Banks.

He glanced over at his communications officer, who had been using *Mohawk*'s bridge computer to link with the Coast Guard's data base ashore. The man shrugged and pointed to a line on the screen. The *Jolly Roger* was indeed listed as a charter boat for Sea View Enterprises, and there were no outstanding violations.

After four years of patrols in south Florida waters, Thomas had acquired a sensitivity that approached a sixth sense, and he would have been willing to swear that the small boat they'd picked up on radar as she crossed the Straits was smuggling, but there was absolutely nothing to confirm his suspicions. He couldn't search the *Jolly Roger* for drugs without a warrant or specific orders from a higher authority. The best he could manage was a check for safety violations, and he had a feeling that with these guys, it would be a waste of time. Their vessel was trim and shipshape, without even a loose line or fender trailing over her side.

He put the mike to his lips again. "Ah, *Jolly Roger*, there are three of you aboard?"

"Negative. We have four. That's two passengers, myself, and one crewman."

"Then I'd like to see at least four flotation devices aboard that craft."

A moment later, the two wet-suited passengers could be seen holding up several life jackets and seat cushions in the light.

"Very well, *Jolly Roger*," Thomas said. "Thank you. Have a pleasant morning and a safe cruise back to port."

"Thank you, *Mohawk*. This is Nan-Sierra-Tango-One-Niner-One-Seven, signing off."

Damn, Thomas thought. He wondered how many real smugglers had made it through into Florida while he'd been wasting time with a charter boat?

Some days, you just couldn't win.

The bottom, Rod knew from his mental chart, shoaled steeply off the south Florida coast, dropping from a few meters to the 100-fathom line—over 180 meters—within a distance of five miles from the shore. The *Jolly Roger* must have made straight for the shallow, coastal waters just off the coast, then swung sharply south. Land—the shoreline of Miami Beach—must be very close, maybe only a few hundred meters to the west. As Rod lifted himself from the raft, he could feel the distant, gentle tug of the inshore current, hear the muffed, far-off thunder of surf.

He looked up.

There was a light up there, a bright one, diffused and scattered by the moving surface of the water. In its backscatter, and under extreme computer enhancement, he could make out twin torpedo shapes, fifteen meters above and perhaps fifty meters away. The *Jolly Roger* had met another, larger boat, and the two had been pulled close together until they were almost touching. The light appeared to be from the larger of the two, probably the glare from a searchlight reflecting off the surface.

As he watched, the smaller craft's engines started up again, and she began moving away slowly toward the south. Almost immediately, the larger vessel's engines picked up their beat, and soon she, too, was moving away, drawing off toward the east and deeper water.

Alone now, Rod decided he would not leave.

He was in no immediate danger. All of his systems checked out normal and functional. His power reserves stood at eighty-four percent, which gave him almost three days at this level of drainage before he would need to recharge. He could walk ashore from here, but the sight of the two vessels overhead had made him pause. The larger one had almost certainly been a Coast Guard vessel. If the *Jolly Roger* had slipped her tow, it had been to avoid being spotted and searched by the Coast Guard.

But five tons of cocaine was an incredible investment. Street values were running $16,000 a kilo now; five tons was eighty million dollars' worth, a staggering amount for one shipment.

For that much money, *Jolly Roger*'s crew would be back, and soon.

He waited.

His inner clock told him it was 0241 hours, nearly three

hours after the sea sled had been cast loose, when the small vessel returned to the area. He was aware of the cruiser's approach first when he heard a faint but clear *ping* echoing through the water . . .

. . . and the raft answered with a shrill ping of its own, followed by another, and another.

A sonar transponder, then, a device set to emit a repeating signal when it received a triggering impulse from the searching craft. The *Jolly Roger* turned immediately and homed on the sonar chirps. In another few moments, he detected the double splash of two men entering the water overhead. Looking up, his optics caught the flash of one hand-held, underwater light . . . then another.

Two men were swimming toward him.

Briefly, Rod considered moving off the raft and finding a place to hide nearby, but he decided not to move. The raft was quite large, heavily loaded, and a maze of struts, straps, and shadowy masses. Unless the divers conducted a thorough search, which Rod thought unlikely, they would not notice him clinging to the framework of the sled.

He was right. One of the men appeared to be carrying a small, portable sonar receiver that let him home in directly on the sled's transmitter, mounted up near the bow. He switched off the pinging, then began gathering up the tow cable, pulling it in hand-over-hand while his partner gave the sled's load a cursory once-over with his light. They worked quickly, the beams from their lanterns stabbing and flashing, illuminating the clouds of bubbles that chortled toward the surface in regular bursts from their tanks.

Minutes later, the two swam back toward the surface, taking the end of the cable with them. In a few minutes more, Rod heard the roar of the *Jolly Roger*'s engines again, the cable drew taut, and then the sled was moving forward, rising until it was once more just beneath the surface.

* * *

On the *Jolly Roger*'s flying bridge, David Colby looked at his luminous watch, then turned and took a hard look to port, searching for the first signs of light in the eastern sky. It was early July, and sunrise was scheduled for 5:15. That was less than an hour and a half off, which meant it would begin getting light soon, but it was hard to tell. Even in the wee hours, the glittering, neon dazzle from the ocean-front condos and hotels lined up along Miami Beach like gigantic glass-and-light dominos washed out the sky.

Escobar, Walden, and Savaiano were going to be furious. Colby just hoped they were still at the rendezvous, because if they weren't, he was either going to have to find a place to stash five tons of coke on his own, or wait for dark again for the run back to Pirate's Cay.

Neither option particularly appealed to him at the moment. Ferré was not the sort to accept excuses. He'd have Colby hunted down and executed just to make an impression on the rest of the small-time smugglers and runners he had in his employ.

He spotted the light at South Pointe Park and brought the wheel over, easing the cruiser into the Government Cut between Fisher Island and Miami Beach. He could see headlights on the MacArthur Causeway now, and the array of freighters, tankers, and container ships tied up at the port authority facilities on Dodge Island. Beyond that, among the rusty tangle of derricks, oil storage tanks, and port industrial complexes, lay the mouth of the Miami River. He kept his speed low as he cruised into the bay, barely leaving a wake in the oily water.

The Miami River empties out of a confluence of canals near Miami International Airport and wanders southeast between the Civic Center and the Orange Bowl, much of it under concrete. The area close to the bay, between the high overpasses of Interstate 95 and Route 1, lies in a heavily industrialized area where freighters tie up at docks beneath loading cranes and smokestacks. A residential area approaches the banks quite closely, however, their front porches overlooking the chain-link fences that keep children from falling in the river. Several of the city's less exclusive marinas and public docks are home to an armada of pleasure craft ranging from dinghies with outboard motors to sleek, half-million-dollar cigarette boats.

Colby turned, studying with a critical eye the line looped over the towing bit on the afterdeck. The cable running into the water was impossible to see at night, and there was not even the ghost of a wake aft to reveal the presence of the sled or its massive cargo. Astern of the *Jolly Roger*, beyond the Route 1 bridge and the Miami Beach condo skyline, the sky was definitely lightening. He'd made it into the river just in time. Any brighter, and he'd be dodging Coast Guard, Harbor Patrol, U.S. Navy, and God knew what else.

"Hey, Ramón!" he called to one of the men with him in the flying bridge. "Make the signal."

Ramón, still rigged out in an orange wet suit, swiveled the *Roger*'s searchlight on its mounting, aiming toward a dimly visible line of docks ahead, at a place where a small and dirty tributary flowed into the Miami from the concrete jungle to the south. A sign, partly lit by a few remaining, functional spotlights, marked the Tamiami Marina. A single light glowed in the predawn twilight at a warehouse above the boat launching ramp.

The *Roger*'s searchlight switched on, then off. Ramón paused, then flicked it on and off three times in rapid succession. In reply, the lone light winked out, then came back on.

"Looks okay, boss," Ramón said.

"Yeah. But keep your eyes open. Escobar'll be pissed

'cause we're late. Tell the others to have their hardware ready."

"Right."

Gently, Colby swung into the marina's turning basin, angling the craft so that, when he cut the wheel sharply right, the submerged sled kept drifting straight ahead until it grounded on the concrete of the boat launching ramp. The *Jolly Roger* drifted up to a vacant pier nearby.

And then the police appeared.

The water was growing lighter with the advancing dawn. Rod felt the metal-on-stone rasp as the sea sled grated against the concrete ramp and came to a halt, still perhaps a meter beneath the surface. He heard the *Jolly Roger* cut her engines and knew that the trip was over.

He rolled free of the sea sled and dropped to the muck of the bottom just below the ramp. The mud clung to his feet and legs, but he made his way across the face of the ramp to the shadowy and dimly seen forest of pier posts and bollards growing in the water close by.

Reaching the shelter of the pier, he cautiously made his way toward the shore, edging forward until his head broke from the water.

And was as surprised as it was possible for a robot to be.

The *Jolly Roger* was moored to a pier on the other side of the boat ramp and was the center of attention for a large number of armed men. Many wore civilian clothes, but four wore the blue uniforms of police officers, and he could see a pair of city police squad cars parked beside the marina's barn.

He increased the sensitivity of his hearing, the conversation coming in crisp and clear above the hollow thump of fiberglass hulls against wooden piers.

"It's about fucking time, Colby!" one of the uniformed

men was saying. "You were supposed to be here three hours ago! What the hell happened?"

"Hey, chill down, Walden," the *Jolly Roger*'s Captain said. "We ran into a Coastie and had to dump the stuff. Then we had wait for the Coastie to leave so we could go back and pick it up. Okay?"

"It's getting light," the police officer said. "We've been squatting in this fuckin' marina all night, and we'll be lucky if half the city didn't see us. C'mon, let's move the shit and haul ass."

A pair of canvas-topped, two-and-a-half-ton trucks were parked behind the barn. Rod heard their engines start, then watched as they were backed toward the top of the ramp. Other members of the reception committee waded into the water not ten meters from where Rod was hiding, found the sunken raft, and began unloading the canisters.

Rod counted five men posted around the marina as lookouts and guards, and another on the rusty catwalk of a nearby city water tower rising above the 7-Eleven that backed up against the boatyard fence. Eight more began unloading the raft, passing the canisters from hand to hand to the waiting trucks.

But Rod's attention was focused on the men in police uniforms. Two had joined the group unloading the raft, while the other two remained on the pier.

Police officers. It took a long moment for Rod to finally accept the obvious. Those men in uniform were either disguised as police officers . . . or they were cops doing some highly illegal moonlighting.

Rod's programmed memories included cases drawn from the history of the drug wars. Among them was information on an incident that had happened quite close to this very spot on the Miami River. In the summer of 1985, several Miami police officers had carried out several drug rip-offs, acting on tips to seize large quantities of cocaine from a smuggler's boat tied up on the river . . . then dividing up the drugs and selling them on the street.

The scandal that broke soon after implicated as many as one hundred Miami police officers in drug rip-offs, sales, and attempted murder . . . and dealt a savage blow to the integrity of the city's police department. Even though the actual percentage of "dirty cops" was something less than one in ten, the effects of such widespread corruption, unequaled since the days of prohibition, were still being felt in the city of Miami years later.

Was he seeing a replay of that incident, or were they using badges and uniforms to confuse or intimidate witnesses?

Rod's memory also included a complete transcript of the Buchanan Report. If those were real police officers gathered on the pier, he could understand how that secret document applied to what he was seeing. The Buchanan Report gave only a few more years before the tidal wave of illegal drugs brought on complete social collapse. Soon, the breakdown of law and order, of society itself would become so great that the country would begin to dissolve. Part of that breakdown, he knew, would be through corruption, as more and more underpaid civil servants, venal politicians, and even law-enforcement officers decided that, since everyone else was doing it, so should they.

And when citizens lost faith in their cities' police forces, that would be the beginning of the collapse Buchanan had predicted.

Rod stared at the blue uniforms and realized that he had to get in contact with Weston or Drake, *had* to. This was a situation that he was totally unable to handle on his own.

🔊Chapter Twelve

ROD LAY FLAT in the shadows between a pair of trash dumpsters in the marina, the radio unfolded in front of him. He was not speaking into the microphone but instead had plugged into the transmitter directly. By splitting the synthetic flesh on his left forearm with a razor-sharp fingernail, and opening a panel concealed underneath, he'd revealed the silvery sheen of a radio jack. Tugging at the jack, he'd popped it free, unspooling a twenty-centimeter cord.

Jack and cord were plugged into a receptacle on the radio's control board now, with the other end of the cable still feeding into the recesses of Rod's arm. He was speaking internally now, manufacturing the radio signals directly and feeding them through the backpack unit in front of him to boost the signal and transmit it.

"That is affirmative," he was saying. "Tamiami Marina, on the Miami River. Estimate at least twenty-five, repeat, two-five bandits, armed with a mix of light automatic weapons, assault rifles, shotguns, and handguns. They have dragged the raft up a boat ramp and are now unloading the cargo and transferring it to a pair of trucks. Over."

"We copy that, Pinocchio," Drake's voice replied, thin and static-scratched through the tenuous radio link. It, too, was inaudible, being converted to words only within Rod's audio processors. "We'll have help there as soon as we can. Over."

"Be advised," Rod said, "that at least four of the bandits are wearing Miami PD uniforms. Over."

There was a long, hissing pause. "Say again, Pinocchio."

"Be advised that at least four bandits are wearing police uniforms. One of them seems to be in charge of the Miami side of the operation."

There was another pause, longer this time. Movement caught Rod's eye. One of the smugglers, a civilian with an H&K MP5 submachine gun slung over his shoulder, had just rounded the barn. He was twenty meters from Rod's hiding place and in plain view. Rod remained dead still. If the man happened to look up, he would almost certainly see the robot where he lay between the dumpsters.

He did not seem to be searching for intruders, however. He took a stance facing the back of the barn, unzipped his trousers, and began urinating against the wall.

"Copy that, Pinocchio," Drake said at last. Rod assumed that Drake was simultaneously in contact with Weston at CIA headquarters, and that the delays included some quick exchanges between Langley and AUTEC. "Langley is making the necessary arrangements to get some help to you ASAP. You just sit tight and stay out of trouble."

"Pinocchio copies. I do recommend that—"

The man with the H&K zipped up his pants, turned, and stared straight at Rod. *"Cuidado!"* he screamed. *"Mire! Mire!"*

"Geppetto, Pinocchio!" the robot called silently. "I have been observed."

He unplugged himself from the radio and slurped in the plastic cable like a strand of spaghetti. The man by the barn was fumbling with his H&K as Rod somersaulted backward, clearing the narrow space between the dumpsters.

Automatic gunfire thundered, slamming bullets into the dumpsters with hollow, steel-gong sounds. One round grazed Rod's left shoulder, tearing cloth and artificial skin, but doing no damage. Bullet fragments embedded themselves in the side of his face.

But the robot was already moving clear of the fire zone, abandoning the radio, swinging his Uzi up, ready to fire. There was another shout nearby, and Rod tracked on the sound, switching to full combat mode. Twin cross hairs appeared on his field of view, one showing where his attention was focused, the other indicating where the Uzi in his hands was pointing.

Another smuggler saw him, eyes widening as he groped for the MAC-11 snugged into his shoulder holster. As Rod raised his Uzi, the cross hairs slid together and became one, centered on the smuggler's forehead. There was a brief, savage crack of sound, and a pair of 9mm bullets tunneled between the man's eyes and out the back of his head, emerging in an explosion of brain, bone, and blood-matted clumps of hair.

Rod pivoted sharply to the left, tracking and firing before the first gunman's body had hit the ground. The Uzi snarled again, loosing a three-round burst that slammed into the chest and shoulder of a smuggler armed with a shotgun, spinning him back into the tire of a huge, four-legged moving crane used to pick up boats and carry them about the yard.

Sounds reached him from the dumpster, the scrape of steel on steel. The man with the H&K who had spotted him in the first place was coming through between the dumpsters.

Rod was waiting when he emerged, the cross hairs already aligned with the dark, steel-walled canyon between the dumpsters, his selector switch set to single shot. He tapped the trigger, sending the 9mm round blasting through the subgunner's right eye. The H&K subgun went off as the gunman jerked back against the steel wall behind him. Rounds snapped through the air . . . but Rod was already elsewhere, moving now at full speed as the thoroughly aroused smuggler band began to close on the sound of gunfire.

There were two main groups of bad guys—the eight who'd been unloading the raft and packing the cargo into the trucks, and eight more talking on the pier. Smaller groups were scattered around the perimeter of the boatyard on guard. Rod saw the man on the water tower raising an M-16 assault rifle to his shoulder, apparently secure in the knowledge that whoever was invading the boatyard hadn't yet noticed the lookout fifty feet above the ground. Rod used his telephoto optics to zoom in on the gunman.

The target was at long range for an Uzi subgun—well within reach of the bullet but too far to allow for decent accuracy. Rod triggered one shot and saw the bullet hole appear in the smooth metal of the tank just above and behind the rifleman's left shoulder. A stream of water blasted out from the 9mm hole. The man turned, obviously surprised at suddenly becoming wet, and Rod's second shot caught him squarely between the shoulder blades, snapping his spine in two and sending him toppling backward over the catwalk's guard rail.

He screamed all the way down, landing with a clatter in the parking lot of the 7-Eleven beyond the boatyard fence.

"The bastard nailed Billy!" someone yelled. "Get him! Get him!"

More gunfire banged in the marina. The men on the ramp were closest to Rod, but only the two in police uniforms had their guns out. The men on the pier were directly beyond the group on the ramp, separated from them by a stretch of water, but they were already scattering, the four who'd been on the *Jolly Roger* diving back into the moored boat, the others pounding along the wood-plank pier toward the barn, weapons at the ready.

One of the maxims of warfare was so basic it had become a cliché: the best defense is a good offense. If Rod remained in one place, superior numbers and superior firepower would sooner or later take him down.

So he charged, racing straight at the men on the ramp so fast his scissoring legs blurred, and a four-foot-tall garbage can that happened to be in his way went clanging across the dock and into the water.

He was in the midst of the first group in less than a second, long before they'd begun to react to his all-out rush. He pivoted left, snapping the Uzi's folding steel butt hard into one man's face, then reversed the swing, plunging his elbow into the sternum of someone to his right. One of the uniformed cops brought his service revolver, a heavy-duty .38, into line with Rod's face. The Uzi *crack-crack-cracked*, bucking in Rod's hands as the sound-suppressed subsonic rounds cratered the officer's chest and stomach.

Then Rod was running again, this time into the closing gap between the two main smuggler groups. He fired another three-round burst, and a man with a CAR-15 stumbled, then splashed into the water. Spinning in place he targeted the first group again, slapping the selector switch to full auto, pumping rounds into the scattering smugglers and into the half-full sea sled drawn up on the concrete behind them. Round after round tore through the fragile aluminum containers, sending geysers of white powder puffing high into the air. Two more men went down as the rest ran for cover or pressed their bellies to the pavement. One got his MAC-11 free of its holster and opened fire with a high-pitched, buzz-saw shriek, sending a stream of 9mm lead into the three men advancing on the run from the pier.

Rod was gone, stepping from between the two groups so quickly the enemy didn't have time to register that he had moved before they were firing into each other. One of the

uniformed men screamed and clawed at his belly, where
scarlet was gushing across blue cloth. The other cop and his
civilian companion returned the fire blindly with a service
revolver and an M-16, snapping shots into the confusion of
smoke and muzzle flashes, striking the gunman with the
MAC-11 more by luck than design and slapping him aside
with bloody holes in his side and shoulder.

Rod's Uzi was empty, the slide locked open. He thumbed
the magazine release, dropping the empty mag to the concrete as he slapped home a full one and snapped the bolt
closed. Gunfire barked from the mouth of the barn and from
behind a forty-two-foot Mercury cruiser resting on concrete
blocks in the boatyard. One bullet slammed into his left leg,
staggering him in mid-stride. Another carried away a snip-
pet of plastic from his right ear. Water splashed and gey-
sered as rounds slapped into the surface from three
directions.

In a single, fluid movement, Rod spun, leaping into the
air and extending his hands, the Uzi still clutched in his
right fist, cleaving the water with a thunderous splash. For
several seconds, bullets continued the rip through the air
where he had been.

Patrol Sergeant Oscar Walden had been on the police
force for twelve years. Never, *never* had he seen any man
move so quickly, shoot so smoothly, or score hit after hit
with such deadly accuracy as had the uninvited guest to the
meet at the Tamiami Marina. It defied reason. Who was this
guy, anyway?

More to the point, who was he working for? As Walden
cautiously approached the boat ramp, his eyes on the dark,
still-churning water where the mystery man had vanished,
the question pounded at his brain.

Walden had entered this deal with misgivings to begin with. Sure, the stories going around the precinct house suggested that everyone was on the take, from the city mayor on down, and morale was at an all-time, rock-bottom low, but that couldn't justify what he and the other men in his squad had gotten into.

Actually, the whole thing had started as a way to get ahead, to score big with his superiors at Division. Rudy Escobar—known as the Eskimo on the streets because he dealt in snow big-time—had been the target of a Vice Squad investigation for almost a year, and it was Walden and other members of his squad who'd finally put the collar on him. For the twelve-year veteran, the final straw had come when the DA had struck a deal with Escobar, letting him walk in exchange for his cooperation as a witness in court at some future date.

The first step toward corruption had been a small one. In fact, it had seemed like a pretty good deal at the time and no dirtier than the DA's arrangement. Walden would ignore the Eskimo's current drug dealing if he would provide names and addresses to Walden and his squad. Escobar had quite a list of "business associates," competitors whom he wouldn't mind seeing put out of business . . . and whose arrests made Walden's record look pretty good.

After that, it had been a short step down to pulling rip-offs of Escobar's rivals, busting them and pocketing half the cash and drugs, or simply stealing the entire load and selling it through the Eskimo's street connections. The deals had been damned tempting for a man on a salary of less than $25,000 a year. In the last two operations, Walden had managed to put aside nearly two hundred grand.

The problem was that most of the money was in shoe boxes stashed under his bed at home. He didn't dare spend more than a fraction of it, couldn't even put it into savings because the bank records would flag any deposit over ten thousand dollars . . . and he'd have one hell of a time explaining that to the police internal security people.

For a long time, he'd been living in dread of being discovered. If there was no way to enjoy the money, what was the point of having it?

Damn it, who *was* this guy, snooping around the marina at five in the morning? The DEA? Miami police . . . maybe Vice? One of Escobar's competitors? His hand was unsteady as it tracked the revolver back and forth, searching for bubbles, a ripple, anything. Where was he?

Escobar stood beside him, training an H&K on the water. "Did we get him?"

"Yeah, Eskimo," one of the others said. "Had to've, man. He just went zap and fell!"

"I'm not so sure," Walden said. "Looked like a dive to me. I don't think we touched the bastard."

The sound of an engine caught their attention. The *Jolly Roger* had cast off her lines and was backing into the turning basin now. "Where the hell are they going?" Marco Savaiano said. Unlike the others, he was, as always, neatly attired in a gray suit. Walden grimaced in distaste and looked away. Perhaps the arrangement with Escobar had begun to go flat for him when he realized who the Eskimo's backers were . . . Mafia hoods like Savaiano.

Damn. The money was great, but he'd do things differently if he had them to do again. "Maybe he swam underwater to the piers over there."

"Lenny!" Savaiano snapped. "Julio! Check it out!"

Two subgun-toting men broke from the crowd and trotted toward the piers. The *Jolly Roger* was standing well out into the river now, her engines stirring a gentle wake. Walden glanced back at the boatyard. it looked like there were bodies everywhere. He counted four . . . five . . . hell, they'd lost seven or eight men at least, and several more wounded. Half the guys who'd walked into the boatyard were dead or hurt bad. A lot of the coke was ruined, too. Trickles of the precious white powder were still draining onto the concrete, blotting up the blood of one of the wounded men.

And Pete was dead . . . and Gonzales. How was he going to explain the deaths of two fellow cops to Captain Mendoza back at Division?

"Hey, the son of a bitch must be dead," Savaiano said. "No guy could hold his breath that long—"

The black form surged up from the water, pillar straight, an explosion of white spray, an Uzi in its hands already blazing into the closely packed cluster of men standing on the ramp less than five meters away. The gunman next to Escobar jerked and fell . . . and then the slugs slammed into Escobar, sending a crimson splatter across Walden's uniform. One of Savaiano's gorillas tried to aim his shotgun, but the deadly hail of 9mm slugs chewed through his belly and cut him down.

Walden fired his .38 revolver and saw water geyser beyond the deadly black shape. He shifted his aim, tightened his finger . . .

. . . and felt something slam into his arm and chest with piledriver force. There was no pain, and for a moment, Walden thought that the blow had been the recoil from his own gun, but then he realized that he was lying on his back, staring into an impossibly blue sky.

Then, slowly, the blue faded to red . . . then black.

Yes, he really would have to reconsider this arrangement with Escobar. Things were not working out right at all. . . .

Rod stood in waist-deep water, hosing the group of drug smugglers with full-auto mayhem. He saw one of the two remaining police officers go down, saw another man stagger, vomiting blood, saw the others scattering in every direction. Two and a half seconds after opening fire, his Uzi ran dry. He tossed the weapon aside and dove into the water again, instants before return fire slapped the water where he'd been standing.

Crawling on his belly, he made his way underwater back toward the shadowy pilings of the pier, surfacing carefully and without a ripple, ready to dive again if he was spotted.

He wasn't. He heard shouts and the pounding of boots on the wooden planks of the pier above his head, followed by shots that probed randomly at the turning basin a dozen meters away. Grasping the piling with both hands, he waited, judging the positions of the men on the pier until they were almost directly overhead.

The piling was slick with a green algae scum, but the robot could exert tremendous pressure, pressure enough to actually indent the tough redwood of the pole as he hauled himself bodily out of the water. Two men stood side by side on the pier. One gasped as Rod levered himself onto the planking, lashing out and grabbing the smuggler's right arm, wrenching him forward and spinning him around, slapping the HM-3 from his hands. The man screamed as Rod's grasp tightened, yanking him back against Rod's torso just as the second man reacted to the robot's unexpected arrival and cut loose with a burst from his MAC-10. The first man absorbed the rapid-fire string of slugs as they stitched him from groin to throat. The bullets were still coming as Rod straightened both arms in an explosive shove that sent the riddled body hurtling up the bullet stream and slamming into the gunman.

Rod followed, his left foot coming down on the MAC-gunner's face with force enough to crush his skull with a bloody, explosive splatter of blood and tissue. Turning and stooping,

Rod scooped up the HM-3, chambered a fresh round, and snapped the selector to single shot all in one fluid chain of movements.

The *Pistola Ametrallador* HM-3 was a Mexican design superficially similar to the Uzi, with a 32-round magazine inserted up the straight pistol grip. It was a lighter weapon than the Uzi, however, and Rod snapped it back and forth through the air several times, recording its handling, mass, and momentum, and adjusting his reactions to the difference. At the same time, he scanned the opposition.

Resistance had broken with that final volley on the ramp. The *Jolly Roger* was racing down the Miami River now, setting up a high, white wake that set smaller moored boats bumping and tugging at their lines. The surviving uniformed police officer was running for one of the squad cars, while three civilians scrambled up the boatyard's chain link fence. Two more piled into one of the Army trucks parked near the ramp.

Standing dead still, Rod sent one 9mm lead messenger crashing into the head of a man in a business suit just as he swung one leg over the top of the fence. The man twisted sharply, then fell backward, one leg becoming entangled in the barbed wire atop the fence so that the body hung head down, jacket tails, arms, and one leg dangling. The other two climbers let go of the fence and dropped back inside the boatyard, unwilling to risk the exposed fire zone above their heads.

The police car bolted from where it had been parked beside the barn, whipping around the corner in front of the barn at full speed just as the Army truck began backing up the ramp and toward the gate. Rod tracked the squad car, squeezing off single rounds one after another. The front windshield crazed, then shattered under the fusillade of shots. The driver's face went bloody . . . and then the police black-and-white was balanced on two wheels, hurtling squarely into the moving truck.

The collision echoed through the boatyard like an explosion, tipping the Army deuce-and-a-half onto its side as the battered squad car crashed and rolled. Gasoline splashed, then ignited. The blast shattered the windows of several nearby drydocked boats, and the fireball clawed into the early-morning sky like a bloated, black-and-orange mushroom. As Rod stepped off the pier and walked across the boatyard, three men appeared from behind a boat, tossing down their weapons and raising their hands. They were joined a moment later by the two survivors at the fence, both locking their hands behind their heads and calling out, "Don't shoot, don't shoot!"

He was still rounding up the prisoners when he heard the faint but rapidly growing thunder of helicopters and the distant keening of sirens.

The first UH-1 Huey flew low overhead seconds later.

◍ Chapter Thirteen

THE COAST GUARD HELICOPTER, an HH-65A Dolphin painted in the Coast Guard's bold red-and-white color scheme hovered thirty feet above the Tamiami Marina, stirring up swirling clouds of dust. Drake leaned out of the open side door, looking down on the battleground.

It was clear that a battle had been fought there. The boatyard was crowded now with police, and the only open space in the entire lot was taken up by a police UH-1 that had settled to the ground near the concrete ramp. Smoke continued to boil from the mangled wreckage of two vehicles, a two-and-a-half-ton truck and what looked like the charred and blackened hull of a police cruiser.

Bodies lay everywhere. Drake could see police officers fishing one floater from the water between two vacant piers with boat hooks. Other bodies were sprawled around the yard, and he could see four sheet-swathed forms lying in a row on the ground. An ambulance had arrived, and men were loading a stretcher into the back. Dozens of police and plainclothes men swarmed among the boats, photographing bodies and the abandoned weapons that littered the ground as thickly as did the corpses, collecting and marking shell casings and other bits of evidence, and cordoning off the large sea sled parked on the ramp. Even from the air, Drake could see the mounds of white powder that had been scattered from punctured cylinders.

According to the report received over the Dolphin's radio, the police helo had arrived at the Tamiami Marina nearly an hour and a half earlier, shortly before Drake had boarded the Coast Guard helo at AUTEC. He'd flown directly across the Straits of Florida to Miami, a distance of 165 miles; during that time, a DEA Clandestine Laboratory Enforcement Team had deployed from the Huey, fanning out across the marina with shotguns and H&K MP5s. CLETs were elite paramilitary forces normally used by the Drug Enforcement Administration to raid illegal drug labs. They were backed up by a sizable contingent from the Miami Police Department, who had arrived with their own SWAT team, ambulances, and a narcotics investigation unit.

It seemed that within moments of Rod's radioed call for help, James Weston at Langley had been on the phone to the DEA's Miami office, formally requesting that an assault force be sent to the Tamiami Marina to back up his agent there. Drake gathered that there'd been some bureaucratic resistance from the DEA agent in charge—understandable enough, perhaps, in light of the continuing rivalry between various government agencies charged with drug enforcement, and especially considering that the CIA had no legal authority within U.S. territory.

Any doubts the local DEA headquarters had had, however, were ended moments later by a second phone call, this one from the President of the United States.

Drake held his headset against his ear and pressed the intercom button that connected him with the Dolphin's pilot. "Can you get me down there?" From where they were hovering, Drake could not see a landing space big enough to receive the Dolphin. The boatyard was full, the nearby streets and the 7-Eleven parking lot made dangerous by parked cars and telephone lines. There were large numbers of spectators, too, passersby outside the marina fence, and people gathered on the front porches of their homes.

"Negative, Lieutenant," the pilot replied. "No space. I don't think you could land a sea gull down there."

"Okay. Look, I've got to get down there somehow. Any way you can manage."

That "any way" turned out to be the chopper's rescue cable and harness. Drake secured the horse-collar harness around his torso beneath his arms, then stepped out the open door of the helo. The Dolphin's crew chief released the winch and lowered him gently to the earth inside the swirl of dust and paper kicked up by the hovering aircraft's rotor blast.

He stepped back onto solid ground a few meters from the barn, slipped off the collar and signaled the hovering helicopter to take it away. He was met by a man in civilian clothes who was very obviously the police officer in charge.

"Inspector Hanley," the man said, scowling. "Are you the spook they said was comin'? Let's see some ID."

Drake flashed his ID, the one identifying him as CIA. While he was not, strictly speaking, employed by the CIA, his Navy assignment to Project RAMROD came under the intelligence service aegis, and often the CIA card gave him access that would have been otherwise denied. "I think you have one of our people here," Drake said. "Tall guy . . . light, wavy hair, gray eyes . . ."

And an infuriating habit of not following his programming, Drake added to himself.

"C'mon," the police officer said. "We got him under lock and key around the corner."

"Lock and key. You handcuffed him?"

"Look, mister. We get this superurgent priority call to come down here and stop what sounds like World War III in the middle of a marina. We get here, flat out, CLET SWAT, police SWAT, the whole nine yards, and what do we find but this guy of yours holding five thugs prisoner at gunpoint. No ID. No badge. And no decent story. Bodies and automatic weapons scattered all over the place, plus three dead cops, and more coke just layin' around than any of us have ever seen in one place in our whole careers! Yeah, you're damned right we cuffed him!"

Drake found Rod patiently lying face down on the ground, his wrists handcuffed behind his back, a uniformed police officer with a Remington shotgun standing guard a few feet away. Drake was so relieved to see him in one piece he grinned at Hanley. "He give you any trouble?"

"Nah. We told him to put down his weapon and he did. But I got to tell you, mister, your pal's in a world of shit."

"What's the problem?"

"Problem? Oh, no problem . . . except that I've got civilian witnesses who saw him shoot four cops, practically on their doorsteps. And to make matters worse, he won't tell us who was with him."

Drake blinked, momentarily confused. "What do you mean, somebody with him? He was alone."

"Aw, fer Christ's sake, man!" He waved his arm, taking in the bodies scattered across the marina, and the ambulance that was just now pulling out the front gate. "Don't you start, too!" He pointed at five men, like Rod, handcuffed and lying on the ground under guard nearby. "So far, I've got five prisoners who say they were ambushed by an army, only there ain't no army around here that I can find. I got eighteen corpses, and three more guys so badly dinged up we don't know if they're gonna pull through! You don't expect me to believe one man took on twenty-six guys by himself and came out without a scratch!"

"Actually," Rod said from the ground, "and as I explained when you apprehended me, the number was thirty. Four men are escaping now in a cabin cruiser, the *Jolly Roger*."

"Shut up. No one asked you."

"Believe me, Inspector," Drake said. "Rod is quite capable of taking on odds of thirty to one and winning."

It was obvious from Hanley's face that he did not believe it. "Look, I've been on the force for goin' on twenty years, now. I know gunshot wounds, and I know ballistics. Most of these stiffs were hit by nine mike-mike, sure, but not all of 'em."

"Actually, I did have help," Rod added. "In a manner of speaking."

"I knew it," Hanley said. "More spooks?"

"At one point, two separate groups of the smugglers were firing at one another. Several of their casualties were from friendly fire."

" 'Friendly fire,' huh?" Hanley shook his head. "Well, now there's another thing. We got three dead police officers here, and a fourth who might not make it. Seems like maybe your friend was a mite indiscriminate when he opened up with that chatterbox he was carryin'. I don't know how they feel about it up in Washington . . . but down here cop killing is kind of a serious offense, y'know?"

Drake looked down at the prone robot. "Rod?"

"The police officers in question were part of the drug-smuggling operation. They met the boat and helped unload the cargo. One of them was clearly giving orders to others."

"Bull shit," Hanley said. "I've known Oscar Walden for years, and—"

"Inspector, if Rod says he saw them dealing drugs, then he saw them dealing drugs. He can't lie."

"Oh, right! I'm supposed to take this bozo's statement, just like that?"

Drake hesitated, wondering how much to say. Technically, Rod's existence and his capabilities were still classified secret. However, the proverbial cat had been let out of the bag months before, when news reporters had witnessed his part in a gun battle on a Georgetown bridge, the battle that had won him the nickname Cybernarc.

So Drake had some official leeway in what he could tell the authorities. WHITE SANCTION had to remain secret, of course, but a great deal of red tape could be avoided if he explained things to Hanley.

"Inspector, I'm afraid Rod is not your typical, garden-variety bozo. He is a highly sophisticated android robot operating as part of a classified antinarcotics program under CIA administrative jurisdiction."

"Right. And I'm Ming the Merciless. Give me a break, Mister! It's been a long day and I ain't even had breakfast yet!"

Drake sighed. "Okay, Rod," he said. "Stand up and give the nice man his handcuffs back."

Rod rolled onto his side, got his feet under him, and stood up. There was a sharp *ping* as he removed his hands from behind his back. With two quick motions, he stripped the locked steel bracelets from his now-freed wrists and handed the twisted metal fragments to the dumbfounded police officer.

"You can send the bill for a new pair to CIA headquarters, Langley, Virginia," Drake said, grinning. He jabbed a thumb at the human prisoners, still handcuffed and lying on the ground nearby. "I would suggest that you interrogate them. I imagine they could give you quite a story about what he can do when he's turned loose." He sobered. "They'll also tell you the truth about those police officers."

"I'll do just that," Hanley said. His voice was low, dangerous.

"We have to get back."

"Hold it!" the officer snapped. "You're not going anywhere. At least he's not! Not until I have some decent answers!"

"Let me use the radio in one of your squad cars," Drake said.

Fifteen minutes later, he and Rod were free to go. Weston himself had gotten on the radio, quoting chapter and verse to the police officer about Federal agency jurisdiction and authority in major narcotics cases.

"But damn it all," the officer exploded as he reached through the window of his squad car to hang up the microphone. "My CLET got called in here for a major bust, and all we have are five prisoners, three wounded, and a hell of a lot of corpses!"

"You also have something like five tons of cocaine," Drake reminded him. "Think what that'll look like in your report!"

"Shit, I'm still trying to figure how to explain all this." He glared at Rod. "And *him*!"

They left the boatyard by way of the Dolphin, which had been hovering in the area all the while. When they lowered the horse collar to him, Rod simply grabbed the cable in both hands and rapidly ascended, moving hand-over-hand with effortless ease while most of the policemen stopped what they were doing to watch. His greater-than-human weight made the Dolphin dip slightly as he reached the door and swung himself aboard. Drake made the trip more conventionally, strapping the collar in place and giving the signal to the crew chief to haul away.

"I'm glad you didn't resist arrest," Drake told Rod once they were both on the deck of the Coast Guard chopper. He looked out the door at the pall of oily smoke staining the morning sky. The entire area seemed to be clogged with police cars and emergency vehicles.

"I am programmed not to resist lawful authority," Rod replied. "But I would like to know one thing?"

"What's that?"

"Concerning those police officers who evidently were working with the drug smugglers. In this case the situation was clear enough. They were part of the force which attacked me, and I was already certain that that force was part of the narcotics operation against which Operation SEA KING has been deployed. But if such corruption becomes commonplace, how will we know who is friendly, and who is the foe?"

"Damned good question, my friend," Drake replied slowly. In modern war, he reflected, it was often quite hard to tell friend from enemy. "And I don't have an answer. All I can say is, when it gets that bad, maybe it'll be too late for us to do anything. The Buchanan Report will have come true."

They passed much of the rest of the trip back to AUTEC in thoughtful silence.

Rod and Drake stepped off the helo at the AUTEC airstrip eighty minutes after leaving Miami. The sleek, HH-65 helo had an operational range of 165 miles, allowing for a thirty-minute loiter on station; the Dolphin was pushing its fuel reserves dangerously close to the limit when it settled to the tarmac at the base air station.

By the time they were down, word had been received by radio that the *Jolly Roger* had been stopped by a Coast Guard cutter twenty miles out of Miami. The *Roger* had been taken in tow, and the four men aboard were in the custody of U.S. marshals.

A military HMMWV—colloquially a "hum-vee"—was waiting for them when they stepped off the helo. At AUTEC headquarters, Commander Baird had already opened a scrambled satellite line to James Weston, who was now en route to Andros.

"I'm aboard RAMROD Mobile One," Weston said over the speaker phone on Baird's desk. "We should be touching down on Andros in another . . . make it three hours, ten minutes."

RAMROD Mobile One was the code name for a government 747, specially equipped with a complete maintenance and repair facility for the RAMROD robot.

"I assume you have both my Combat and Sea Mods embarked upon the aircraft," Rod said.

"You assume correctly," Weston replied. "We're ready to move Operation SEA KING into high gear. Ferré must be taken out."

"Ferré has his own army on Pirate's Cay, Mr. Weston," Drake said. "Are you still planning on bringing in the Marines?"

"Affirmative," Weston said. "We still have to get specific clearance from the Bahamian government first. Possibly we can employ island constabularies and make this an international effort."

"May I make an observation?" Rod asked.

"Of course," Weston replied. "You're part of this thing, too."

"I feel constrained to point out that there is a high degree of probability that Carlos Ferré has agents acting on his behalf within the Bahamian government."

"How do you know that?" Drake asked.

"It seems self-evident. The fact that he has made considerable land purchases on Pirate's Cay with little opposition or official notice, many of them presumably at the expense of resident islanders, suggests that he has friends at court, as it were."

"Makes sense, Mr. Weston," Drake said. "If he could buy Florida cops, he probably has a Bahamian bureaucrat or two in his pocket as well."

"There is also the possibility that the crew of the *Jolly Roger* was able to warn Pirate's Cay of the debacle in Miami before they were apprehended. In short, gentlemen, we must consider the possibility that Ferré has been warned of our victory in Miami . . . and will almost certainly learn of our plan to attack his island as soon as the matter is raised in Nassau."

"Well," Weston began. "A few hours warning won't—"

"God, he's right," Drake interrupted. "The hostages, Mr. Weston! The hostages!"

"You don't think he's going to start shooting them, do you?" Weston asked. "Dead hostages are of no value to him."

"Predicting Carlos Ferré's reactions to our deployment is difficult," Rod said. "However, he has many hostages, if we include in their number the civilians still on Pirate's Cay. He has at least some of the women and children locked up in the Strand, and others would be easy targets, especially if there is some delay in getting the necessary permission to deploy combat troops in the region."

"And he'd certainly be willing to shoot a few just to prove he means business," Drake said. "Sir, we can't wait for approval from Nassau! We *can't!*"

"So what do you suggest we do?" Weston wanted to know.

"I should think that was obvious," Rod said. "We should insert a team onto Pirate's Cay as rapidly as possible in order to secure the hostages' safety."

"Well, there is a problem there," Weston said. "The Bahamian government has been cooperating with us for some years now, and they've been taking a hard-line stance against drugs. As Lieutenant Drake pointed out a moment ago, if we launch a military operation in their waters without getting their permission, there could be . . . unfortunate diplomatic consequences."

"Screw the diplomats," Drake said bluntly. "We've got a hundred people on that island who could get blown away if we don't do something, and fast."

"Agreed. But you don't just walk in and invade another country."

"There's precedent," Drake said. "Operation URGENT FURY was primarily aimed at rescuing American medical school students on Grenada before they could be rounded up by the local thugs in power."

"The Bahamas are not Grenada," Weston replied. He looked thoughtful. "Much of our drug interdiction effort is based in the Bahamas. Make them mad enough, and—"

"Well, we can't warn them we're coming. One word in the wrong bureaucrat's ear in Nassau, and Ferré'll be waiting for us, with bells on."

"If I might venture a suggestion," Rod said. "I have been on the island. I know the layout, and the disposition of forces. If you were to send me back onto Pirate's Cay, I might be able to secure the release of the hostages, then keep them safe until the Marine force could secure the necessary permission and land."

"That could be tight. Not to mention illegal."

"In what way is a covert operation on the island to save American and Bahamian lives more illegal than the covert reconnaissance operation I have already conducted?"

"He's got a point there," Drake pointed out.

"I'm afraid he does."

"This time," Drake added, "I don't care what Pinocchio here says, he's not going in there alone."

"Agreed," Rod said. "In this instance I will appreciate the support of additional firepower."

There was a long silence from the speaker on the desk.

"Commander Baird?" Weston asked at last.

"Yes, sir," Baird said.

"Notify your Marine CO. I want them ready for a combat drop inside of twelve hours. Lieutenant? Rod?"

"Yes, sir," Drake replied.

"Rod's argument makes sense."

"You are sending us in?" Rod asked.

"Damned right," Weston replied. "You boys are going to secure the civilian hostages. Then the Marines can go in and kick some drug-smuggler ass."

⟨⟩ *Chapter Fourteen*

UNLIKE HIS OTHER INCARNATIONS of Combat or Civilian Mod, Sea Mod was not a separate body for Rod's computer and sensor housings, but an extension designed for his Combat Mod housing. The unit actually looked much like a one-man sea sled, a black-painted, cut-away torpedo powered by water jets instead of propellers. Instead of a control panel or steering controls, the streamlined swelling at the torpedo's bow was shaped to receive Rod in Combat Mod.

Fifteen minutes after RAMROD Mobile One touched down at the AUTEC airstrip, Dr. Heather McDaniels and five technicians from Project RAMROD's programming and maintenance teams had Rod strapped down on a stainless steel table in the 747's sterile, white operating theater, removing his head and what in a human would have been his heart and lungs—the cylindrical, steel-and-ceramic bundle that housed the robot's central computer core, memory, and control processors. His Civilian Mod body, minus the head, was taken away to be hung up like an old suit, while the black Combat Mod armor was swung into place on a chain hoist. The chest and shoulders unfolded to receive the computer core.

It took an hour or so to make all of several hundred connections of wiring, power cables, and sensor feeds. Then the bulky, humanoid giant was hoisted into the air once again and lowered into position, face-down, on the Sea Mod platform. His arms, shoulders, and helmeted head were inserted into the sled's forward cowling, which clamped down with the sharp hiss of hydraulics and pressurized air.

Rod was unable to move now on his own. The complete assembly, with Rod included, weighed just over 1,000 pounds, and he was quite immobile with his legs strapped to the aft deck of the torpedo. The Sea Mod was gently lowered onto a weapons cart, which was trundled down the 747's tail ramp and wheeled across the tarmac to the jacked-up belly of a Navy SH-60B Seahawk helicopter.

Two flanges, like wings on either side of the sled, were unfolded and locked into position, then slid into both the port and starboard hardpoints on the helicopter's fuselage.

Normally, those hardpoints carried Mk-46 antisubmarine torpedoes, each weighing 568 pounds. With the sled in place, it looked like the helo was carrying some kind of black, flat-bodied, delta-winged aircraft.

Minutes later, they were airborne and heading north, with Drake and his equipment inside, Rod slung from the outside. It was, Drake reflected, a somewhat undignified way for the robot to travel, but it certainly was efficient.

Space inside the Seahawk was cramped. The SH-60B was a LAMPS III aircraft designed for ASW and electronic warfare. What would have been a cargo deck in a transport chopper was jam-packed with computers, radar screens, magnetic anomaly displays, and wiring. The SH-60 normally carried a crew of three, with no room for passengers, but on this flight the sensor operator had been left behind to make space for Drake and his gear.

He'd drawn weapons and equipment from AUTEC's armory. Most of it was already sealed inside a special cargo compartment built into the Sea Mod's deck. Drake wore camouflaged combat fatigues and a scuba rig. His boots, combat harness, and Uzi all were stored aboard the sled.

He slipped on a radio headset. "Pinocchio, Pinocchio, this is Geppetto," he said. "Do you copy?"

"Geppetto, Pinocchio," Rod's voice replied. It was strange to think that the robot was only centimeters beneath Drake's bare feet, slung from the belly of the helicopter like some kind of bomb. "I copy."

"How's the ride out there?"

"An interesting perspective. Much like an airdrop, but with considerably greater wind pressure, of course. My external sensors are working at optimum. I can see clearly out to a range of approximately forty miles. Our objective is already in sight at the limit of my resolution."

Plugged into the Sea Mod's external sensors, Rod could see and hear, as well as employ other, less human senses, even though his head and much of his torso had been swallowed up by the large device. Drake tried to imagine what it would be like having a "body" so different from the one he normally wore, and failed.

"Weather is clear, visibility unlimited," Rod continued. "I see numerous surface pleasure craft, but none which indicate a threat to our mission."

"Copy that, Pinocchio. Just hang on until we get to the DZ. Then we'll see what they have in the way of threats."

"Hey, Lieutenant?" the Seahawk's pilot called over the helo's intercom. Drake could see the pilot and his copilot/tactical officer in the cockpit a few feet away, but the rotor noise made the IC line necessary. "We got a priority scrambled for you. Line two."

"Got it." He flicked a switch on the communications panel to which his headset was linked. "Puppet Master, this is Geppetto."

"Geppetto, this is Puppet Master," Weston's voice said. "I have some bad news."

Drake felt his gut go tight. Surely they weren't aborting the mission! They couldn't. . . .

"Go ahead."

"Our chargé in Nassau just reported some stiff opposition from members of the prime minister's cabinet. They are refusing to allow us permission to conduct military operations in their waters."

Damn!

He heard Weston's sigh, muffled and flattened by the scramble encoding to a toneless hiss of air. "We're continuing to talk with them, trying to bring them around. However—"

"Puppet Master, Puppet Master," Drake interrupted. "Say again. Repeat, say again last."

"Geppetto, this is Puppet Master. There has been a setback in our talks with the Bahamian—"

"Puppet Master, Puppet Master, your transmission breaking up. Repeat, your transmission breaking up. Can you hear me?"

"I hear you fine, Lieutenant. I suggest you stop the act and—"

"Puppet Master, Puppet Master, I do not copy. We are Charlie Mike, repeat, Charlie Mike." *Continue mission* . . .

"Lieutenant!" Weston shouted. "Don't—"

Drake yanked the plug, then opened the intercom line to the pilot. "Radio silence from now on, guys. Don't acknowledge any calls."

"You got it, Lieutenant. We're coming up on . . . make it thirty miles from the DZ."

"Roger that. Keep me posted."

He began to check his scuba gear and other equipment.

What he had just done—ignoring James Weston's priority

transmission, cutting the RAMROD director off in mid-sentence—would very likely get him a court martial. Or would it? Drake might be a Navy SEAL lieutenant, but Weston was CIA, and RAMROD a CIA-controlled operation. Would Weston throw him back to the Navy for court martial, or would it be a civilian trial? For that matter, would there be a trial? Drake knew a very great deal about RAMROD and WHITE SANCTION that the government no doubt would like to keep hidden from the public at large.

It bore thinking about.

But Drake already knew what he had to do.

The innocents . . .

Unbidden, the memory of the bedroom of his Virginia Beach home, of its transformation into a bloody-walled slaughterhouse returned with paralyzing force. He'd come home from work as usual and walked into a trap. The sight of the pale and gore-splattered bodies of Meagan and Stacy tied to that bed filled his brain, gnawing at him, a living nightmare that went on and on and on. . . .

His wife and daughter had been seized by members of a Hispanic street gang. *Los Salvajes*—the Savages—they called themselves, but Drake knew they were nothing but gutter scum, street punks caught up in something much bigger than themselves, working for a narcotics ring operating in the Norfolk-Washington area. He'd killed the butchers himself, but that had done nothing to end the nightmares, the loss, or the driving, burning lust for vengeance that turned his nights to hell . . . or made his days worth living. The real butchers in that room had been the men of power and money and corruption behind the street punks, men who'd long ago sold their souls for bank accounts in the Bahamas and the Cayman Islands filled with narcodollars.

"Comin' up on the DZ, Lieutenant."

"Roger."

He unsnapped his safety harness, stood up, and slid open the SH-60's side door. The helicopter was rushing across dazzlingly sunlit-waters twenty feet above the surface. Drake could see the helo's shadow etched against the clear waters below.

This, he thought, was all he had left. Each mission with RAMROD was another chance to strike back at the bastards who had robbed him of everything he loved.

The situation was ironic. He'd been so bent out of shape over Rod's independent-mindedness . . . but his actions were far worse. There was a distinct possibility that Weston would not be able to send in the Marines, that he and Rod would die on Pirate's Cay, and the hostages with them. Two men, after all, would not be able to hold off Ferré's entire army for long.

But Drake could not stand by and watch the monsters win.

"Stand by to release package," the pilot said, interrupting his thoughts. "On three . . . two . . . one . . . *now!*"

The three-meter-long, black wedge shape detached from the Seahawk's torpedo rails. Drake felt the upward surge of the aircraft as a half ton of weight dropped away, saw the shadow of the sea sled part from the helo's shadow as it plunged toward the water. Leaning forward in the door, he caught a glimpse of the Sea Mod instants before it struck the water with a tremendous splash.

"Package away," the pilot reported. "Telemetry okay. We've got a signal."

"Your turn next, Lieutenant," the copilot/tactical officer announced.

"Roger. Thanks for the ride."

"Any time, Lieutenant. Write if you find work."

Drake detached himself from the radio headset as the Seahawk turned, then slowed, descending until it was less than fifteen feet above the water. He made his final equipment check. While a helocast was not as dangerous as a paradrop into the sea, anything loose could easily be torn away by the impact when he hit the water, and he had no jump master but himself to look for loose fittings or improperly secured gear.

Satisfied, he stood barefoot in the door and leaned against the wind, his swimfins looped by their straps over his left arm, mouthpiece clenched between his teeth, right hand squeezing his mask tight against his face.

He stepped into the air.

An instant later there was a shock, and he was engulfed by a vast cloud of white bubbles that dispersed rapidly as he sank beneath the surface. Doubling over, he pulled on his swim fins. By the time he'd checked his airflow and cleared his mask of water, he was aware of a looming presence to his left. Rotating in place, he saw the blunt nose of Rod's Sea Mod, approaching slowly just beneath the surface, looking like a small whale or some improbable monster of the deep.

Almost affectionately, Drake reached out and patted the Sea Mod's torpedo-sleek nose. Nothing Weston could say or do could reach them now.

He and Rod were going in . . . together.

When he was strapped into the Sea Mod's steel embrace, Rod's senses were far different from those he used with his other, more human bodies. He still had sight and hearing, of course, but his vision was sharply restricted now, and both his infrared and telescopic enhancements were almost useless. Rod's normal hearing was helped somewhat by the density of the water—sound waves travel faster and farther in water than in air—but the sounds were distorted, difficult to track . . . and most were meaningless in any case, the creaks and pops of shrimp and crabs and other noisy sea creatures.

There were no surprises as he scanned the undersea world. He'd tested the Sea Mod already in a tank at the Farm, and data on its operation had been downloaded into him before he and Drake had come to the Bahamas. In many ways, traveling underwater in Sea Mod was the same as it had been during his nighttime ride across the Florida Straits, only with him in control of their course, with better visibility, and without the chilling danger of dropping into the inky depths hundreds of meters below. In one sense, though, Rod had actually become the submersible that was cruising now a few meters beneath the surface.

In Sea Mod he had built-in sonar. Besides detecting sounds in the water, he could emit shrill, sonar pings that gave him range, bearing, and even the approximate size and composition of targets ranging from fish to the sandy sea floor itself. Though not as sophisticated as a dolphin's sonar, Rod's electronics could sense the waters around him with fair accuracy.

He'd picked up Drake as soon as the SEAL had helocasted into the sea. Switching on his water jets, Rod veered toward his human partner. It took only seconds for Drake to swing onto Rod's back and grab the handholds set on either side of the sled's platform. Two swift pats on his Combat Mod armor told him that his passenger was ready, and Rod swung his prow toward Pirate's Cay, shifting his engines to full ahead. He'd been tracking the island even as he dropped from the SH-60; at thirty knots, they would reach the island in less than twenty minutes.

The pressure of the water began building along his flanks and prow as he surged ahead through the sea.

The aircraft was a twin-engine Piper Navajo, one of the small fleet of aircraft Carlos Ferré used to smuggle loads of cocaine and marijuana forth from Colombia, through airbases in western Cuba, and into the Bahamas. Aboard were a veteran pilot and one of Ferré's Cuban soldiers. Their mission was sentry duty. They'd taken off from the cay's airfield an hour earlier, and they'd been circling the island ever since, searching the crystalline blue waters and white beaches for any sign that the seclusion of Pirate's Cay was being broken by intruders.

Ferré had seemed quite insistent that the *norteamericanos* were going to try something, and very soon. His threats kept both men alert, scanning the waters below carefully.

"Allá!" the Cuban snapped, pointing. "There! There is something!"

The pilot pulled the Navajo into a sharp bank as he peered past the Cuban's shoulder. "Shark," he said. *"Un tiburón."*

"I think not." The Cuban showed his teeth as he reached behind his seat, fishing for the large, canvas satchel he'd brought with him on the flight. "Call Vista del Mar and tell them we have a sighting. Give the location. Then take us back over that 'shark' once more."

The pilot shrugged and did as he'd been told. There was a sudden, sharp rush of wind. The Cuban had pulled back the lever and opened the door slightly. In one hand he clenched a round, metal sphere painted a bright candy-apple green.

"Hey!" the pilot shouted. "What the hell are you doing?"

"Bombing." He had already pulled the cotter pin free and held the grenade in his left hand, keeping the arming lever closed. With his right hand, he held the door open against the wind, squinting down at the water. "Lower . . . lower . . ."

"Get rid of that thing! Are you crazy? You could get us both—"

"Be quiet, please. You disturb my concentration. A bit slower . . . slower still . . . there!"

His arm snapped convulsively, hurling the Russian-made hand grenade straight down toward the water. The Navajo banked sharply and he craned his neck, watching for where it would land.

There was a thunderous crash, and a pillar of white foam vaulted into the sky.

"Qué bueno! . . . "

Rod had sensed the grenade's impact on the water and known at once what it was. For several seconds, he'd been puzzling over a low-frequency sound he could not identify that seemed to be emanating from above the surface. The appearance of the grenade revealed the mystery: a light aircraft was circling overhead, and their invasion of Pirate's Cay had been discovered before it had properly begun.

WHAM!

The detonation slammed them with a wall of steel-hard water. Rod was rolled almost onto his side by the force of the blast, and he could feel Drake clinging desperately to handholds on his deck.

There was no way to communicate with his passenger. RAMROD planned an upgrade that would allow underwater communication between divers and the Sea Mod . . . someday. In the meantime, all Rod could do was veer sharply away from the roiling disturbance of the underwater detonation and push his speed to the limit. By his calculations, the beach was less than two hundred meters away.

If they could survive long enough to reach it.

His sensitive hearing detected the approach of the aircraft's engines once more. Holding his course until the last possible moment, he suddenly swung sharply right, hoping to throw off their attacker's aim by a last-second maneuver. He heard the plop of a steel sphere hitting water twelve meters away. . . .

WHAM!

Closer that time. Several of his audio sensors were gone, and Rod wondered how Drake was managing. The shock waves of a close, undersea blast could kill, as any dynamited fish could attest. Rod knew that his structure could probably survive a near miss, but Drake was flesh and blood, subject to concussion, ruptured eardrums, unconsciousness, and death.

Unable to discuss the situation with Drake, Rod's mind shifted rapidly through several alternate courses of action. Behind them all was the realization that Drake tended to get upset when Rod made a decision without consulting his human partner.

But consultation was out of the question now. The airplane was coming around for another pass.

◉ Chapter Fifteen

ROD DECIDED ON A STRATEGY. The light aircraft circling overhead could obviously see him; his black, torpedo shape must be clearly visible from the air, when seen against the sunlit sands in clear water only a few meters deep.

He had to keep them from dropping grenades close to Drake. Since he was the main target, the logical course of action was to dump the SEAL and draw the enemy's fire.

Rod increased his speed. He felt Drake's fist thumping on his back, one-two-three, a signal they'd agreed meant *wait* or *be careful*. Deliberately, Rod rolled on his left side and turned hard to the right, adding centrifugal force to the rush of water past his flanks . . . and suddenly the pressure of Drake's body against his back was gone.

His speed increasing now, Rod arrowed toward the beach. From the air, it might be apparent that a swimmer had just been dropped off, but the attackers would surely concentrate their attention on him for the time being.

WHAM!

The explosion rocked him violently, and his starboard wing dragged against the sand. He felt the tug of the surf . . .

. . . and then his belly scraped bottom as Rod beached himself at better than thirty knots.

Surf broke across his partly exposed back. With his prow wedged into the sand he could not move, an easy target for the aircraft's next pass.

But the robot was already initiating release commands, separating himself from the Sea Mod's embrace. Sensor connectors detached themselves from receptacles in his chest, momentarily blinding and deafening him as his contact with the outside world was broken. There was a hiss as pressure seals opened and magnetic clamps unlocked. Backing out of the space shaped to receive his head and torso, snapping shut the panels on his chest that had been opened to effect the Sea Mod linkage, Rod again was aware of himself as himself, a two-meter-tall man-shape in matte-black titanium steel.

Standing waist-deep in the water alongside the grounded sled, he could see the aircraft pulling around in a sweeping turn a half mile out over the ocean. Clearly it would be coming back for another pass in seconds. There was no sign of Drake.

He moved quickly. Bending over the surf-washed sled, he released four catches and opened the Sea Mod's storage locker. Several large waterproof bundles were strapped inside, but Drake's Uzi and several grenades had been clipped to the hatch where they could be retrieved in a hurry.

Rod shifted his attention to the Piper Navajo. With telescopic enhancement he could clearly see two people in the cockpit. The man in the copilot's seat had the door cracked open and seemed to be holding something in his hand . . . probably another grenade.

Rapidly dwindling numbers appeared on his visual field to the right of his targeting cross hairs as Rod shifted to combat mode. He probed the target with a radar pulse. Range was now less than 500 meters, with a closing velocity of 80 meters per second.

The robot faced a difficult decision, one which had to be made with superhuman speed. The aircraft would be within effective range of the Uzi within four seconds; by timing his shot, he could empty the 32-round magazine into the aircraft as it approached.

But there were too many variables to be certain his volley would bring down the Navajo. Fired head-on at the approaching aircraft, the bullets would disperse no matter how careful his aim. Worse, the pressure wave ahead of the Navajo would deflect the light 9mm rounds—or at least rob them of a fair amount of their kinetic energy. Rod estimated that perhaps half of the bullets could be expected to miss, or hit the aircraft's hull at such extreme angles that they would glance off harmlessly.

And those rounds that did score solid hits would do so randomly, sent tumbling by each bit of metal or wiring or foam insulation that they hit. They *might* do fatal damage to the aircraft or even kill the pilot . . . but it was more likely that they would not.

The aircraft had to be brought down now, and he needed heavier firepower to do it.

Rod reached into the equipment locker and grabbed, not the Uzi, but one of the hand grenades.

Massing .39 kilos—over four-fifths of a pound—the M33 fragmentation grenade was a dense, lead-shelled sphere the size and shape of a baseball. Keeping both eyes and radar fixed on the approaching Navajo, Rod pulled the cotter pin and released the arming lever.

The shot was a difficult one, even for a robot with computer targeting, radar ranging, and telescopic vision. He had to compare the aircraft's 264-foot-per-second approach with the expected velocity of the grenade when it left his hand, match the trajectories of aircraft and missile, balance the grenade's fused time delay with the time it would take the Navajo to close the range. . ..

Juggling mathematical variables with lightning speed, Rod

counted off precisely 1.96 seconds, then hurled the grenade with an echoing whipcrack of sound. . . .

The Navajo pilot could see the big guy in black standing next to the submarine, or whatever it was, just off the beach. The sight sent a shiver down his spine. The guy was just standing there, as unmoving as a statue, and it made him think of all the rumors he'd been hearing on the cay about giant black monsters who tore men to pieces with their bare hands.

Then the thing's arm blurred. . . .

There was a shrill clang from the nose, and the aircraft yawed. *We've been hit!* flashed through his mind. Numbly, he felt the Navajo's rudder controls go soft as his feet moved the floor pedals uselessly. His eyes widened when he glanced down and saw a yawning hole between the Cuban's feet where something large and heavy had smashed through aluminum hull, insulation, control hydraulics, and the bottom of his passenger's seat. . . .

He looked at the Cuban and felt sick. *"Oh, shit! . . . "*

Rod counted off the seconds as the Navajo continued to approach, and then the explosion blew out the aircraft's windows and filled the cockpit with flame. An instant later, the entire aircraft erupted in a savage, orange fireball as the fuel tanks ruptured and blew, spewing smoking fragments of metal across a wide arc of the sea. A large, flaming mass hurtled low over Rod's head and smashed its way through the trees behind the beach, as two severed wingtips and a piece of the rudder fluttered through the sky like the scattered petals of a flower.

Moments later, a tall, dripping figure emerged from the water, swimfins and mask in one hand. Rod grabbed handholds on the side of the Sea Mod sled and began dragging the massive hull further up onto the beach.

"The threat has been neutralized," Rod said matter-of-factly as Drake approached. The SEAL was scanning the sky and the nearby forest as though expecting another attack. "I have scanned the area. We are secure."

"Yeah," Drake said, eyeing the robot hard. "Why'd you ditch me out there?"

"Without communication there was no alternative. Since I was the principal target of the attack, I felt that the best strategy was to distance myself from you, while simultaneously reaching a point where I could separate from the Sea Mod, secure a weapon, and return fire. I have done so." Rod hesitated. What was his sometimes unpredictable human partner thinking? "I realize that you would prefer that I consult with you before taking specific action. However, you must realize that there are times when the tactical situation precludes such discussion."

He waited. Drake's face was creased by an expression which Rod could not immediately recognize. Was it anger? Frustration?

Suddenly, unexpectedly, Drake burst out laughing.

"Is there something about the situation you find amusing?" Rod asked.

"It's not you, Rod," Drake said when he recovered his breath. "It's me. Here I was, about to tear into you for saving my life, and for knocking down a hostile aircraft. I guess sometimes we humans can be a bit less than rational!"

"I have noticed." Rod scanned the treeline quickly. Smoke was boiling into the sky from the spot where the Navajo's wreckage had crashed. "I suggest that we get the Sea Mod under cover and equip ourselves. The locals may decide to take interest in our activities here."

Together, they began to drag the sled up the shelf of the beach.

* * *

They were a *team*, a close-knit combat team unlike any seen before in the history of warfare.

The realization struck Drake full force as he helped Rod unpack the rest of their equipment, then hide the sea sled under a blanket of fronds and branches well back among the trees. They'd saved each others' lives more than once and were used to covering each others' backs. Drake was still not sure what it was that motivated the RAMROD robot— why Rod seemed to address each mission with a more-than-machine-like dedication and intensity—but he knew that he didn't have to know.

He knew only that Rod was worthy of his trust.

His scuba gear had been stored in the sled's equipment locker. He'd retrieved boots, combat harness, and boonie hat, along with his Uzi and a backpack heavy with 9mm ammo. Rod was busily unpacking his primary weapon for the op, spreading it out on the ground like the parts of a gigantic and lethal-looking puzzle.

Designated the XM-214, the weapon was popularly known as the six-pack. It was a smaller version of the M-134 mini-gun, a portable Gatling gun with six, rapidly rotating gun barrels driven by a power pack strapped to Rod's back. The weapon had been modified so that Rod could carry it slung from his shoulder, but together with its power pack it still weighed over thirty kilos, and its 1,000-round ammo cassettes weighed thirteen kilos apiece. One human could never have carried that load for long without dropping to his knees, but Rod shouldered it easily, the heavy weapon looking like a large and complex toy in his grasp.

Drake helped make the final adjustments, strapping two ammo cassettes to each side of the robot and making sure that the belts of 5.56 fed smoothly into the weapon's receiver without tangling. He had just completed the task when Rod turned, scanning the jungle. "I hear several vehicles approaching," he said. "Range 200 meters and closing. They may be investigating the crash."

"We're clear here," Drake said. They'd policed the area as they worked, and Drake had already made certain that the deep tracks in the sand where they'd dragged the Sea Mod had been erased all the way down to the water line.

Silently, man and robot faded into the forest.

Armando Estrada was shaking as he delivered the news to his old friend. Carlos had become even more unpredictable these past few days, even more paranoid. Aside from rumors and nightmare stories, though, there was no tangible threat.

But the rumors of a monster, of a robot of unbelievable strength and power wreaking havoc among Carlos's people, were spreading like wildfire.

The rumors did nothing to calm Estrada's state of mind as he searched for Carlos at the airfield. The Piper Navajo had radioed only that something had been spotted in the waters to the east and then it had gone down. Did that mean that Cybernarc was already on the island?

He found Ferré outside the airfield's small tower. "It is true, Carlos," he said. "They found the plane, crashed in the forest. Muñoz says he does not believe it was an accident. It looks like there was an explosion inside the cockpit."

Ferré did not appear to hear. Carefully, keeping his back to the breeze off the sea, he sprinkled a line of white powder on his hand, above the base of his hand, raised it to his nose, and snorted noisily. When he turned and looked at Estrada, his eyes were burning like twin coals. "So, my old friend. The final attack has begun, *si?*"

"I . . . I'm not sure I know what you mean, Carlos." He

tried to read his friend's expression but saw there only anger
. . . and lurking fear, barely held in check.

"Cybernarc," Ferré said softly. "Cybernarc is here. He
destroyed our shipment in Miami, and now he is here
again."

"We don't know that."

"You may not," Ferré snapped. "I do. Our source in
Washington says that our entire load was confiscated in
Miami. The *Jolly Roger* has been captured by the Coast
Guard. Several of our people are in custody, others are dead.
Cybernarc!" The word was spoken like a curse.

"What are you going to do?"

"We are going to wait for it. At the villa. Come with me."

Still trembling, Estrada followed his old barrio friend
toward his limousine.

Rod was still in battle mode, with red cross hairs in his
field of view next to the rapid, numerical flicker of ranges,
bearings, and other necessary data. He would have preferred
to make the assault at night. He'd been designed as a night
fighter, for darkness conferred advantages on the black-
armored robot no human could experience.

But he had the combat advantage by day as well.

Extending his vision into the infrared, he allowed the
false-color heat images of the guards to overlay his normal
vision. He counted twelve guards in sight around the Strand:
two by the front gate, four on the upper floor balcony, six
more scattered about the grounds or on the columned porch
in front of the building's lower floor.

The greatest danger was the penetration of the 5.56mm
rounds spewed by the six-pack. The guest-cottage facade
was constructed partly of cement block, partly of wood, with
large windows and doors that were probably no more than

two thin layers of plywood sandwiching a couple of centimeters of air. If his estimate of the situation was correct, there were hostages behind those doors, probably dozens of them, and one of them a U.S. representative. He had no wish to rescue the civilians by killing them with friendly fire.

He opened his tactical radio channel, speaking silently with an internal voice. "Geppetto, this is Pinocchio. In position."

"Copy, Pinocchio. Go." Drake was forty meters away, like Rod hidden in the pine trees surrounding the Strand. The tactical, voice-activated radio headset he wore allowed him to communicate with Rod but left his hands free for the task at hand.

Which was to watch Rod's back.

The robot switched on the Gatling gun's power. The barrels began to spin with a high-pitched whine. That was another calculated trade-off. The loss of complete surprise would be more than compensated for by the weapon's sheer shock effect. The nearest targets were the gate guards ten meters away, visible as shifting heat images behind a screen of ferns and tropical pine boughs.

Rod stepped into the open.

The two sentries were slouched against the bole of a massive tree, one with his M-16 slung, the other with his FN-FAL leaning against the trunk. Both were just looking in his direction, no doubt wondering at the source of the whine, when Rod stepped into view, the XM-214 already tracking. He squeezed the trigger and the whine became a howl, a shrill cacophony like a buzzsaw shearing through steel.

One part of Rod's mind tallied rounds as he fired them, and watched the steady drain on his internal power. If the six-pack had a major disadvantage, it was the way it devoured ammo. A selector switch let the rate of fire be adjusted to either 400 or an incredible 4000 rounds per minute, and he had it cranked to the highest setting, knowing that the weapon's shock value was worth it. Spitting sixty-six rounds each *second*, the bullets flew practically nose to tail, a solid stream of lead that chewed through everything in its path with spectacular effect.

The man with the M-16 came apart, his torso vanishing in a bright red fog. His partner, stooping to pick up the FAL, lost most of his body from his chest up, as splattering gobbets of meat and bone, hair and clothing, blood and brain mingled with white splinters of wood gouged from the tree in a hailstorm of lead.

Rod shifted aim, walking the nose-to-tail stream of slugs into a guard twenty meters beyond the tree. Bullets slammed into the man's spine, snapping it in three places, mangling the body as it fell in a twisted, bloody heap.

His finger came off the trigger as the barrel tracked past the body and onto one of the guest-apartment windows. He broke into a run, pounding through the gate and past the steaming, chopped-meat ruin of the gate guards, rushing the building in a frontal charge that left the surviving defenders momentarily stunned. The XM-214 snarled again, shredding through a guard and the wooden pillar behind him like a swinging chainsaw. He moved again, shifting his line of aim to bring his next target clear of an apartment door, then fired again, the burst picking the man up, shaking him in midair, and flinging him down like a bundle of wet laundry.

His audio sensors detected a muffled rattle to his left, and one of the sentries on the balcony doubled up over the railing, then dropped four meters to the ground. The rattle sounded again, and a second balcony guard staggered, slammed against the wall at his back, and collapsed. Drake was picking and choosing targets from cover, dropping men who were so thunderstruck by Rod's charge that they didn't even realize they were being cut down from two directions at once.

Two bullets screamed off his right shoulder, another from

the massive armor plate of his helmet. Pivoting, he shredded that gunman, then shifted aim to three more running for the fence, sweeping them down in a splattering one-two-three.

A third man fell from the balcony, drilled by Drake's carefully placed fire from the trees. The fourth balcony guard dove for a stairwell, taking shelter where the steps were between him and Rod. An instant later he discovered that an inch or two of pine provided insufficient protection from that leaden hailstorm that chewed through steps, handrails, wooden balusters, risers, and stringers as though they were made of paper. The guard and his AK-47 crashed through the wreckage in an avalanche of splintered wood.

Rod paused long enough to check his power supply. Still okay. Normally, the XM-214's battery pack could only charge the weapon for about 3000 rounds, but a special modification allowed the battery to draw power from Rod's internal fuel cell chargers, extending its life and increasing its efficiency. The downside, of course, was the drain on Rod's available power, but the sheer, mind-numbing volume of firepower in that portable Vulcan cannon made the trade-off worthwhile.

He kept moving, closing now on the building. By Rod's count, all twelve of the guards posted outside were down. The weak point of the plan, of course, was that there was no way to guess how many guards there might be inside the apartments. During his earlier visit, he'd seen men entering and leaving those makeshift jail cells freely.

One of the doors opened. . . .

A man burst through the doorway, barefoot and shirtless, an AK-47 blazing away in a sustained burst that sent rounds smashing into Rod's chest and torso, pounding at him with a sound like hammered boilerplate. Rod snapped his weapon around but held his fire. This new target was directly in line with the open door.

Then Rod heard a woman's scream, and a kicking, struggling shape came through the door. It was a second gunman, shielding himself behind a shrieking, naked woman. He held her close, his left arm locked across her torso beneath her breasts, his right arm cocked high, pressing the muzzle of a Beretta automatic pistol against her skull. "Don't shoot!" the man yelled. His voice cracked, betraying panic. "Don't shoot, or my girlfriend here is dead!"

The gunfire ended abruptly as the two half-dressed gunmen with their helplessly struggling prisoner advanced toward where Rod was standing.

◉Chapter Sixteen

"TWO TARGETS," ROD TOLD DRAKE with his inner voice. "Priority Alpha with the woman. Priority Beta to his left. You take Beta."

"Affirmative," he heard Drake reply in his head. "Three . . . two . . . one . . . *fire!*"

Alpha was hunched down, his head and torso almost completely screened by the girl's body. He'd made one obvious mistake, however, and that was to leave his gun hand and most of his right arm exposed above the woman's right shoulder. It *looked* dramatic, but . . .

Drake's Uzi snarled, the burst catching the AK gunner from the side. In the same instant, Rod triggered the spinning, whining Gatling.

The six-pack howled. Rounds crashed into the back of Alpha's hand, shattering his wrist, snapping the Beretta's muzzle away from the woman's temple in an eye's blink. The gun fired and the woman screamed again, clutching her ears, but the bullet missed her forehead by three inches at the same moment that round after round shredded the gunman's arm in a splintering whirl of bone chips and meat. Rod held his radar on the bullet stream, sensing where each round passed within inches of the woman's head, careful not to let the scything stream of death touch her.

The hostage dropped face down on the ground, leaving her captor standing above her, shrieking as he clutched at an arm that was suddenly missing from the shoulder. His severed hand continued to grasp the pistol on the ground beside her.

From the trees, Drake loosed a follow-up burst into the wounded man, who was dead before he hit the ground.

Rod stepped forward, the Gatling smoking. He reached down and helped the shaken woman to her knees. "Is your room empty?" he demanded.

"W-what?" She seemed lost, dazed. Her nose was bloody, either from the concussion of the Beretta going off in her face, or from the shock wave of the Gatling bullets. Probably her hearing was affected as well.

Rod repeated the question, his voice booming from the black helmet.

"Yes," she managed to say. She was trembling, showing signs of going into shock. "Please . . . who *are* you?"

"A friend. Come inside." It was an order which permitted no argument.

Drake joined them moments later. "Fourteen up, fourteen down," Drake said from the doorway.

"There may be others hiding among the hostages," Rod said. "We must—"

His hearing picked up a piercing shriek of pure agony.

"What is it?" Drake asked. The sound had been too faint for human ears.

"Someone in pain," Rod replied. "It sounds like a man."

Drake's eyes widened. "Rutherford! Let's go!"

They left the rescued woman wrapped in a blanket and lying under her bed, warning her to stay down. The scream had come from another of the ground floor apartments, and as they approached they heard it again. Drake's face was pale.

They hit the door together, Rod's powerful forearm smashing the door in a flailing spray of splinters. Drake went through low, rolling on the carpeted floor, Uzi up and ready.

It had been a man's scream, but the scene was not what they'd expected. Instead of finding Rutherford, they found two more hostage women, standing above the nude body of another smuggler sprawled on the bed. Apparently, when the gun battle had begun, one of the women had turned on her captor with a nail file; the other had managed to smash a bathroom mirror and finish him with one of the shards. There was a great deal of blood.

One of the women faced Rod steadily as he entered, her eyes wide at the sight but her face set and unflinching. She took in his black armor, the monster six-barreled cannon in his hands. "Thank God, you're here at last!" she said. "You're SAS, of course. . . ."

"Negative," Rod said. The islanders must have been hoping for a rescue by Great Britain's elite commandos, the Special Air Service.

"We're Americans," Drake explained. "Stay inside, and stay down. We'll let you know when it's safe!"

"Like hell," the other woman said. She retrieved a Browning Hi-power automatic pistol from the floor beside the bed where their captor had dropped it. She yanked back the slide clumsily, but with a thin-lipped determination. "We've had just about enough of these bastards!"

Elsewhere in the building other women were emerging, many with children, as the word spread from apartment to apartment that their guards were dead. Several women appeared in the doorway. Rod could hear shouts outside as the word spread. "It's the U.S. Marines!" and "It's the SAS! They're here!" He could hear cheering in the yard.

Within several minutes it was clear that the last of Ferré's men at the Strand was dead, that the hostages were hostage no more.

But Rod and Drake were on the verge of losing all control of the situation, and the robot did not know what to do about it.

Drake shook his head firmly, hands planted on his hips. "Listen up, ladies! Listen to me! We appreciate the offer, but you can't just go charging out there with guns blazing!"

"Those bloody bastards have held us here for weeks!" one young woman yelled. She wore a brilliantly colored Blackbeard's Castle T-shirt and carried a baby in her arms. "Doing what they like, raping us, beating us . . . I say we beat *them!*"

"Yeah!" several others chorused.

"Then you're going to do it in an orderly and proficient, military manner," Drake barked. "You!" He pointed at the woman holding the pistol in a bloody hand. "Grab five or six people. Go through every room in this building. Make sure everyone is okay. Any sign of the bad guys, you call us. Got that?"

"Yes, sir."

"Anyone here know first aid?"

"I'm a doctor," one woman said.

"Go with them. See if anyone's hurt. You. Grab as many people as you need and start picking up guns. You know about guns?" A vigorous nod. "Make sure they're on safe. Collect any ammo you can find, too. . . . "

Drake continued giving orders, and soon the mob of women and children had become, well, not disciplined, but at least it had become a mob with purpose.

"Anybody here see a man, an American?" Rod asked. "Or his wife? A blond woman named June?"

"I think I heard one of the guards say that there were other people up at the villa," one woman volunteered.

"Somewhere upstairs. We haven't seen them here."

Which meant that there were more hostages to rescue, calling for a raid on Ferré's villa fortress itself. That was not a pleasant prospect.

"We should tell the men that we're okay," the woman with the gun suggested. "If they knew we were free . . ."

"Are there telephones here?" Drake asked.

"They were all torn out when Ferré's men brought us here."

"I can call them," Rod announced.

"Do it," Drake ordered. "Just make sure you're talking to someone who lives on the island, not one of Ferré's men. Have him pass the word that the women and kids are safe."

"Shall I have them assemble here?"

"If they can get away, sure. But I don't want them starting any pitched battles with the bad guys. If Ferré's men are around, they should lie low and wait."

Drake continued passing out assignments, taking charge simply by giving orders in a strong and authoritative voice rather than making suggestions. More often than not, the tasks were make-work, but with something to do the women would be less likely to get in the way. He didn't want parties of civilians wandering into firefights, or getting picked up again by Ferré's army.

But they would have to act quickly, before enemy forces, alerted by the gunfire, could react.

Getting in contact with the men in Windsor had been a surprisingly simple task. Rod's internal radio could access the local radio-telephone service, based to the north on Grand Bahama. When he and Drake had been standing in the bar called the Royal George, he'd noticed a pay telephone on the wall. By replaying that scene from his memory,

Rod could focus on the telephone, computer-enhance the image, and read the number that was printed in the center of the old-fashioned dial.

He read that number to the radio-telephone operator, and moments later he was speaking directly to Sammy, the bartender at the Royal George.

The first visitors to approach the Strand had been a pickup loaded with Ferré's men. Whether they'd come to investigate gunfire and were expecting trouble or were simply coming to replace the guards or visit the women was unknown. Rod was standing guard at the time on the roof of the apartments, and he sent a searing blast of rapid-fire lead into the vehicle as soon as he could zoom in on the cab and verify that all of the occupants were, indeed, members of Ferré's army.

The windshield exploded. An instant later the engine followed, as a fireball of flaming gasoline erupted from the fuel tank. The burning wreckage rolled over and over across the road, finally coming to rest upside down.

Twenty minutes later, the first of Windsor's men began arriving at the Strand, driving vehicles of all descriptions, carrying weapons liberated from those of Ferré's men whom they'd been able to catch. Preliminary reports suggested widespread confusion throughout the southern end of the island, as Pirate's Cay's men, no longer held captive by the knowledge that their wives and sweethearts were prisoners, turned on the drug runners with a ruthless and unrestrained vengeance.

The sudden rising gave Rod a lot to think about. This was clearly one of those situations Drake had mentioned a few days earlier, where the robot had been unable to anticipate a purely human reaction. Rod had not known how to control the near riot of the women at the Strand, had not been able to predict the response of the men in Windsor. His human partner had understood it all, however . . . though Drake admitted that even he hadn't expected the revolt to be as vicious as it was. A number of islanders had been killed in widespread fighting, but the vast majority of the casualties were Ferré's men, and the battle was spreading fast.

Rod continued to mount guard on the apartment building's roof. Drake joined him, his Uzi slung over his shoulder. "Seen any more of Ferré's men?"

Smoke from the wrecked pickup was still staining a brilliant blue sky.

"Negative, Lieutenant," Rod replied. "Reports suggest that the southern end of Pirate's Cay has been for the most part liberated. Ferré's men are retiring to the villa, either to escape or to make a last stand."

"How can they escape?"

"There is a small landing on the west side of the island, below the villa. When I last reconnoitered the area, a vessel of the type known as a 'cigarette boat' was moored there."

"Ferré's getaway," Drake agreed. "Okay. We've got to get in there before they decide to kill the Rutherfords . . . or take them somewhere else."

"Agreed. We should also make provisions for securing the safety of the former hostages." Rod hesitated. "I confess to some concern. By ignoring Mr. Weston's order to abort, you may have left the entire task to us. We cannot expect the U.S. Marines to land on Pirate's Cay as we originally planned."

"No," Drake said. "We can't. But we can radio Nassau. The police. The Government House. Whoever you can reach. Let them know that a large group of civilians have freed themselves from—um—call it 'pirates.' Tell them the people need help—food, water, medical attention—and tell them that you're radioing the story to the local newspaper there in Nassau . . . and to the American embassy."

"Why refer to the media?"

"Insurance. I don't know how many people in the Bahamian government are in Ferré's pocket but I know they'll keep a damned low profile if the press already has the story. Maybe all they'll send is a boatload of local constables . . . but they'll send someone. These people need help."

"And us?"

Drake sighed, looking toward the east, toward the sea. "Well, like you said. We can't wait for the Marines anymore, right? So we'd better get on and do it ourselves."

Rutherford sat on a cot in a darkened room, his hands cuffed at his back. From the panic he'd seen among his guards he was sure that he was about to be killed. The shouts registering faintly through the walls of the small upstairs bedroom suggested that something was happening.

And then there were the gunshots he'd heard an hour earlier. Rutherford had been an infantryman in Vietnam, and he knew the sound of assault rifles and high-speed auto cannons. Was there an assault under way? He could only sit and hope, speculating on whether or not a rescue force could get to him before Ferré shot him out of hand.

And what had they done with June? "By God," he muttered half-aloud. "If they so much as touched her . . ."

The door to his room banged open, and one of the guards appeared. He gestured, and another man shoved June into the cell. She'd been given military fatigues several sizes too large for her, and she wore straw sandals on her feet. She was handcuffed but appeared unhurt.

"Clyde!" she called, her face brightening. "Clyde! You're okay!"

The guard grinned down at them, and Rutherford stiffened.

This was it. He wondered if he could throw himself at the man, knock him down, maybe buy time for June to flee. . . .

"Okay, lovebirds," the guard said. "You stay put until the Chief decides what to do with you."

The guards left the two Americans alone in the darkened room, banging the door behind them.

"You okay, Junebug?" Rutherford asked. This was the first time he'd seen her since they'd been separated days before, and he found he was trembling. He'd been ready to sacrifice anything for June, his career, his honor, his life, if necessary . . . and here she was, alive and at his side again. Tears streaked his face.

She fell against his shoulder. "I'm okay. They . . . they made a lot of threats, but they didn't hurt me. Oh God, Clyde! What's going to happen?"

"I don't know, hon. I think a rescue might be under way. We'll just have to wait and see."

But there'd been no sounds of gunfire for some time now, and that was discouraging.

"What are the cement mixers for?" Drake asked. He lay on his belly in the woods, pressing the binoculars against his eyes. The rear of the villa was a beehive of activity. It looked like Ferré's men had just completed pouring a large amount of cement into the foundation of the house, and the work crews were dismantling the chutes and water hoses now, their job, whatever it was, complete.

"Unknown, Lieutenant." The robot, of course, needed no binoculars. "However, their defenses seem to be in considerable disarray."

Small groups of soldiers trotted across the grounds. Drake could see one guard on a second-floor balcony, and a pair of empty trucks parked beside the building, suggesting that there were more troops hidden inside than out.

Carlos Ferré must be a very worried man by now, Drake thought. The reports from Windsor could not be good, considering that at least twelve to fifteen of his men had been caught by the enraged citizenry there and either been killed or beaten senseless. And he'd not be reestablishing contact with the Strand. They'd left two locals in charge there: Angie Preston, the woman with the Browning Hi-power, and Samuel Barris, the bartender at the Royal George. Barris had led ten men from the town in through the front gate, all of them carrying weapons that still bore the bloodstains of their former owners. When Drake and Rod had left for the villa, the civilians had been cheerfully organizing their defenses, passing out more weapons captured from Ferré's thugs.

That part of the operation, at least, had gone smoothly. There remained the problem of finding Rutherford, his wife, and the other woman Armitage had mentioned. After that, there was the matter of running down Carlos Ferré. SEA KING was a WHITE SANCTION operation; Ferré had to be killed or captured, and from what Drake had heard about the treatment of the civilians on Pirate's Cay over the past weeks and months, he had little interest in capturing the man for trial.

Ferré was an animal, and he would die.

"How are we going to get in there, Rod? A hundred meters of open ground, and machine guns inside the house. You could rush them like you did at the Strand . . . but that might give them too much time to kill their hostages."

"Surprise would be useful," the robot replied. "You could pass as one of their soldiers now in your fatigues, though perhaps an olive-drab uniform would be better. I, on the other hand, may have a problem becoming inconspicuous."

"Hate to tell you, Rod, but you're about as inconspicuous as an M-1 tank in a china shop." His eyes narrowed as a third truck approached the villa, eight or ten troops crowded into the back. "But if we can get some wheels, we might just be able to remedy that."

"Excuse me. Wheels?"

"Come on. You'll see."

Ferré and Estrada were coming down the stairs when Muñoz hurried toward them from the back of the house. *"Jefé!"* the Cuban called. "There have been reports of more gunfire."

"Donde?"

"On the road between here and the town. And the rumors . . ."

"What rumors?"

"That Cybernarc is here . . ."

"Pah! Cybernarc! Has anyone seen him?"

"No, *mi Jefé.*"

"A pity. Because if he were here, I could prove once and for all that no piece of American military technology can out-think a *man!*"

He heard a shout from outside and moved from the stairs to a window, moving the curtains aside to look out.

Another of the village trucks he'd appropriated had just arrived in front of the building. The wooden slats that had protected its flatbed had been shot to bits, the deck swept clean of all but splinters and a loose bundle of canvas. The windows were gone, the door had been punctured by a dozen rounds, and a splash of blood still glistened on the side of the cab. The driver, the truck's only occupant, staggered as he dropped from the cab. He wore a Cuban's army uniform and carried an Uzi slung over his shoulder.

Ferré had given the order for all of his men to return to Vista del Mar hours before, right after he'd learned of the disaster in Miami. They'd been coming in all morning, most of them piled into the back of trucks like that one. From the looks of things, this truck had been ambushed on the road, probably by machine guns.

Several men had gathered around the driver, who was describing what had happened to the truck with expansive sweeps of his hands. But who were the attackers? DEA? American Marines?

Or the thing called Cybernarc?

"Muñoz!" he snapped suddenly. "Go upstairs and get our guests. I think I want them to be close by me until we know the situation better."

"*Si, señor.*"

"And you, my old friend," Ferré told Estrada. "Come with me. Quickly!"

⚡ Chapter Seventeen

ROD HAD RIDDEN UP THE HILL slung from the belly of the truck, securely tied to the suspension by loop after loop of heavy rope. From his hiding place he could hear Drake opening the door, could see the SEAL's booted feet as his partner climbed out of the cab and began describing a ferocious encounter with an unknown enemy on the road from Windsor. He spoke English, pretending to be one of Ferré's American employees, a driver who had escaped the ambush by driving straight through, not stopping as the autofire volleys from the woods killed the other men riding the truck.

The story Drake was telling was not far from the truth. A truck *had* been ambushed on the way to Vista del Mar and eight men had died in the space of three bloody seconds. The only departure from reality was the notion that the driver had survived. He had not, but Drake had taken his place after tying the robot under the truck.

"You'd better tell them inside," one of the guards told Drake. "Everybody is going crazy in there."

"Right away," Drake said. "You know where can I find Señor Ferré?"

"*Momentito,*" another man said. "I do not believe I have seen you before. . . ."

186

With a flick of each wrist and ankle, Rod snapped the ropes holding him in place, then lowered himself gently onto his back. *"Qué pasa?"* someone asked. On the ground, Rod rolled onto his stomach, then dragged himself toward the villa, away from the cluster of feet where Drake was ringed in by smuggler troops.

Once out from under the truck, Rod stood erect, a towering figure of black menace. One man stood a few meters away, and Rod advanced on him with the relentless power of a freight train, reaching out, plucking the AK-47 from nerveless fingers, then smashing him back-handed across the hood of the truck with horrifying ease.

"Madre de Dios!" one Cuban soldier standing on the villa's front porch screamed. Other men looked, some groping for weapons, others scattering in panic. Rod's borrowed AK crackled, cutting down a pair of guards just rounding the corner of the villa.

The men around Drake had decided to scatter, evidently believing themselves to be entirely too close to the monstrous, black apparition rising from behind the truck. Drake opened up with his Uzi, spraying death in savage bursts that were neither as accurate nor as spectacular as hellblasts from the robot's six-pack, but that hacked running men down with more than adequate efficiency.

Rod, meanwhile, hurled the AK at an advancing Colombian gunman with deadly savagery, smashing his skull. He whirled then, reaching beneath the pile of canvas on the truck. The XM-214 was hidden underneath, together with its ammo packs and battery.

The six-pack whined to life, then shrieked. The *cubano* standing at the top of the porch steps had just managed to get his H&K MP5 unslung and aimed at the robot when the six-pack howled, lifting the guard off his feet, slamming him backward into the white-painted, ornately decorated double doors of the villa. Those doors dissolved in whirling chips of wood as he crashed through, the bullets plunging through them and the mauled body as thickly as raindrops.

Rod paused long enough for Drake to reconnect the battery pack and help secure the ammo cases, and then he was crashing up the steps and through the shattered doors. Inside the marble-floored entryway, the six-pack caught a Colombian coming down the stairs in a hash of blood and splattered tissue. Then Rod swung, catching the crew of a Soviet-made machine gun set behind a sitting room window from the side. They screamed, struggled, and died under that deadly hail.

More men burst into the entryway, armed with automatic weapons. Rod's six-pack continued to shriek, hacking down man after man in a bloody slaughter. One terrified face registered in Rod's computer memory: Vargas, the "doctor" who had performed Ferré's filthy work in the basement. He was unarmed, begging for mercy, but the shrieking stream of lead scythed through his fat body in the same instant that Rod became aware of him, exploding it in a gory spray.

A soldier beside Vargas dropped, clutching the floor, but apparently unhurt, the last survivor of the aborted rush. "Don't kill him!" Drake snapped. "We need a live one!"

Rod took three steps and dropped one massive hand to the man's shoulder. He struggled in Rod's grip, trying to bring his MAC-10 to bear, but Rod increased the relentless pressure. Bones snapped beneath steel fingers. The gunman screamed, dropping his weapon.

"Donde están los Americanos?" Drake yelled at the writhing man. *"Digamé!"*

"Don't hurt me!" he shrieked in English. "Don't hurt me!"

"Tell us! Where are the Americans?"

"Allá!" He gestured up the stairs. "Upstairs . . . to the right . . ."

Gently, Rod picked up the discarded MAC-10, held it balanced on the palm of his hand, then squeezed. The weapon's frame deformed like clay. Rod dropped the ruined weapon in the man's lap. "Thank you," he said. "Remain here."

"*S-si!*" the injured man squeaked.

The stairs protested under each step that Rod took, but he reached the top, scanning walls and doors with infrared vision. He could not always see through walls, but if plywood walls or plaster were thin enough, he could occasionally pick up the heat shadows of people moving on the far side. There were three figures behind the door of a room at the top of the stairs. Rod went in, ignoring the door and crashing through the wall instead in a white avalanche of plaster dust. His maneuver completely surprised three Colombian gunmen hiding inside, their automatic weapons trained on the door.

Rod's Gatling gun shrieked, scattering body parts and broken weapons across the room.

Drake came in behind him and they agreed to split up. Drake would take the hallway to the south, while Rod went north.

Down the hallway and around a corner, a lone man with an H&K subgun stood outside a bedroom door. The XM-214 snarled once, showering spent brass off the wall to the robot's right and cutting down the guard. Rod advanced again, had almost made it to the door when it opened, and June Rutherford came out.

Rod recognized her at once, though her face was strained and tear-streaked, and she was wearing baggy and misshapen military fatigues. Her hands were bound behind her, and a man was moving carefully at her back, keeping her body between himself and the robot's Gatling.

"Stop! Drop the weapon! *Pronto!*"

He recognized the voice, Sergeant Muñoz, from the torture room in the basement.

This situation was far worse than the confrontation outside the Strand apartments. June Rutherford's captor was taking care not to expose any part of his body that could give Rod a clear shot or a chance at a quick kill. He kept his weapon hidden, the muzzle pressed into the back of the woman's head, while his left arm encircled her throat. The hall was narrow . . . too narrow for any kind of flanking movement.

There were simply no options that he could see.

"Your weapon!" Muñoz said. "Put it on the floor!"

Rod did as he was told, his sensors fixed firmly on what he could see of the man. "What is it you want?" he asked, taking a step closer.

"Hold it there, monster! Not another step!"

Rod stopped, less than a meter from June and her captor. He could see partway into the room from which the two had emerged. Clyde Rutherford stood inside, hands behind his back, his face twisted by a terrible, burning rage.

"You, I presume, are Cybernarc?" Muñoz said evenly.

"I have been called that."

"I've been waiting to meet you. You will follow us downstairs now. No false moves, or I will shoot the girl."

Rod could see past June and Muñoz well enough to make out the top of a stairwell. Muñoz wanted Rod to follow him . . . but where? And why? There were no answers.

"Good-bye, Señor Congressman," Muñoz called. "We will be certain to keep your June safe for you until you complete our little task for us, okay?"

"You fucking bastard!" Rutherford screamed from inside the room. Rod caught the movement in his peripheral vision, of the American politician lunging toward Muñoz head first, his hands locked behind his back.

It was precisely the distraction Rod had been looking for. The pistol wavered, then swung from the back of June Rutherford's skull, extending past her right shoulder and taking aim at the charging congressman. For one stark instant, both the pistol and the hand grasping it were completely visible.

Rod's left arm lashed out, delivering a blow that audibly cracked through the air. The heel of his hand struck the Beretta, driving it sideways into the wood of the door frame a few inches behind it. Rod's arm kept driving, snapping the door frame and embedding pistol and hand deep inside the tortured wood. Muñoz shrieked and released June Rutherford, his left hand grasping his right wrist as he tried to pull his mangled hand from where it was buried inside wood and plaster.

There was a popping sound as bones snapped, and then the pistol, flattened by Rod's pile-driver blow, clattered to the floor. With it fell four crooked, pink-and-red objects— Muñoz's fingers, severed when the pistol's grip pulverized his hand.

The effect was as though two tons had descended on his hand in the space of a palm's breadth. Blood spurted in arterial pulses from the ruin of Muñoz's wrist. He sank to his knees, still screaming. Then Rod's fist popped into his skull like a pencil through an eggshell, silencing the screams forever.

Drake came running up from behind. "Congressman!" the SEAL called. "Are you all right?"

"Yes, thank God! Who are you?" His eyes widened at the sight of Rod, who was peeling open June's handcuffs as effortlessly as he'd freed his own wrists at the Tamiami Marina. "Or should I say, *what* are you?"

"Project RAMROD, Congressman. We're here to get you out."

Rutherford turned when Rod approached him, holding his hands out so the robot could strip off the handcuffs. When freed, he rubbed his wrists gratefully.

"Cybernarc," Rutherford said. He looked up at the looming, black machine. "There's a guy downstairs who wanted to know all about you."

"Yeah, well, we have a date with that guy, Congressman. Maybe we can all become better acquainted."

"He . . . he's a monster," Rutherford said. The congressman was panting hard, his face chalk white as he took June into his arms. In trembling, tumbling phrases, he described the murder of Mike Foss, the rape-murder of Foss's wife, the threat to do the same to June if he did not cooperate.

"What did they want you to do?" Drake said. His voice was subdued, but Rod heard the deadliness behind the words.

"They wanted to know about this guy, for one thing," Rutherford said, nodding toward Rod. "And I think he wanted me to be his man in Washington. Or one of them. The bastard has his claws in other people on the Hill, I think. He bragged about how somebody there was passing him information."

"Lieutenant," Rod interrupted. "While this is enlightening, I suggest that we get them to a safe place. The battle is not yet over."

"My partner here is right," Drake said. "Congressman, I want you and your wife to stay in one of these rooms. Get down on the floor and stay there until we come for you."

"Okay," Rutherford said. He squeezed June again, then released her. "Unless you need another gun?"

"Negative, Congressman," Drake said firmly. "We came here to get you out, not have you get shot in a firefight!"

"Understood. But . . ." He looked at the two rescuers uncertainly. "Surely there are more than just the two of you?"

"We hope that reinforcements are on the way," Rod said. "But if they are not, we will have to handle Ferré's men by ourselves."

The congressman looked down at Muñoz's crumpled, broken-headed corpse. "Well, God help Ferré's men, then."

"Hell, I don't think God is going to have anything more to do with the guy," Drake said.

Ferré had heard the gunfire upstairs, had heard Muñoz's screams—abruptly stilled—and knew the Cuban was dead. Cybernarc would be here looking for him at any moment.

"We can reach the boat, Carlos," Estrada said. "We can be in Cuba before they know we're gone!"

"I have a score to settle with this machine." Ferré's eyes darted about the room. It was a large, sunny room, a lounge with broad windows overlooking the sea. It seemed far removed from the horrors of gunfire and death. An expensive oriental rug graced the wooden floor, and expensive bronzes rested in niches along the walls, among potted plants and expensive furniture.

Everything was ready, *waiting.* . . .

"Hey, man," Estrada said. "I'm not gonna just sit and wait for that thing to come to get us!"

"That, my old friend, is precisely what we are going to do." He drew a pistol from his waistband, a Beretta M92S, and chambered a round.

"What, face that monster? No way . . ."

The Beretta cracked in Ferré's hand. A look of uncomprehending shock spread across Estrada's face, as his hands closed over the spreading red stain on his belly.

"Sorry, *old friend,*" Ferré said with an unpleasant smile. "But I need you here. I was going to use one of our guests as bait, but you will do just as well."

The bedroom adjacent to where the two Americans had been held was empty. They left the two rescued hostages there, lying together beneath the bed. Drake had just given Congressman Rutherford the dead guard's H&K when he heard the crack of a shot.

"Downstairs," Rod said, looking up. "Single round, nine millimeter."

"Are the Marines here?" Drake asked. "Or one of Ferré's people got nervous?"

"The latter, I would think. We should investigate."

"I'm with you."

The villa's defenses seemed to have collapsed. Rod gunned down one panic-stricken drug smuggler on the stairs, but most of the members of Ferré's small army appeared to have simply dropped their weapons and fled. The quick, hard strike at the villa itself seemed to have broken the defenders' spirit.

"Ayudamé!"

Drake broke into a run, following the sound of a cry for help. Rod followed closely.

Toward the back of the house, a small, disheveled man with a mustache sat on the floor, cradling the head of another man who was obviously seriously wounded. "Help me," the first man said, looking up at Drake and Rod as they entered. "I . . . I surrender. Only please, help my friend!"

Drake checked the room quickly. No one else was there. The pictures, the furniture, the large carpet beneath their feet all seemed perfectly in place.

"I am Carlos Ferré," the man added. His eyes were riveted to Rod's bulky form. "I surrender! But Armando here, he is my friend! Years . . . years ago, we were children together in Medellín! Please . . . could your powerful machine carry him?"

Rod started forward.

"Stop!" Drake snapped. His left hand swept out, smacking against Rod's chest. "Don't move, Rod!"

The robot froze in place.

Drake took two steps . . .

. . . and felt the rug suddenly give way beneath his weight. He was falling, falling through a large hole hacked through the floor. The oriental carpet had been tacked over it with nails, but the weight of a large man—or of the far more massive robot—was enough to send him plunging into the basement.

He hit something that splashed, a cold, wet clamminess that clung to him in the darkness like thick mud. He smelled sand and water. Irrationally, the first thing he thought of was quicksand . . . but what would quicksand be doing in the villa's basement?

Acting on that first instinct, though, he spread his arms and legs, distributing his body's weight. The carpet beneath him helped. Drake looked up toward the ragged circle of light five feet above his head. He heard a thump, and then Rod's head and shoulders appeared in the hole.

"You appear to have fallen into a trap," the robot said. "One meant for me."

Drake spat gunk. "Get me *out* of here, you overgrown can opener!"

Rod vanished, then reappeared a moment later. Something darkened the hole as it dropped through. A moment later, the battery pack for Rod's Gatling gun dangled by its straps two feet above Drake's head.

He managed to pull one hand free and grab hold. The other arm followed, though the movement drove his legs deeper into the semisolid muck.

Rod pulled. There was a terrible sucking pressure . . . and then the robot was hauling Drake up out of the trap, pulling him through the hole in the floor, helping him scramble to safety. The stuff clinging to every part of his body was like gray mud. Rod rubbed some between two fingers and gave his pronouncement. "Cement," he said.

"A basement room full of wet cement?"

"An elegant trap. I am now overlaying the floor plans I have recorded of this structure." There was a pause. "Yes. The basement room where I saw construction taking place is located directly beneath this room. They cut a hole in the door to receive the chutes through which cement was poured from those trucks we saw. No doubt, all doorways in that room have been sealed and strongly reinforced. My mass is considerably greater than yours. I would have sunk straight to the bottom, and I very much doubt that even my strength would have been sufficient to pull me free. There would have been no leverage, and I would have been blind and deaf as well."

"Well, I sure as hell couldn't have pulled you out. Thanks." Drake sat up. The wounded man lay by himself on the other side of the hole. "Where's Ferré?"

"He fled as soon as you fell. I could not both chase him and extricate you."

"Yeah," Drake said. Again, the robot had made a choice . . . and saved his life. "Thanks . . ."

There was nothing to be done for the wounded man. When Drake reached him a moment later, his eyelids fluttered once. "Carlos always was a bastard," he said. Then he died.

Rod was standing very still. "What is it, Rod?"

"I am picking up radio transmissions from close by," the robot said. "They are encrypted. Something is happening."

"I should damn well think so," Drake said. He was staring out one of the windows now, toward a crystal-blue sky. A C-130 Hercules was passing low over the island, and from its rear door ramp flowered blossom after white blossom. "Parachutes!"

Outside, moments later, they watched as the first paratroopers touched down on the grassy sward around the villa. There were some distant sounds of muffled gunfire, but here at the villa, most of the drug smugglers were already dropping their weapons and raising their hands. A second C-130 droned overhead, followed a moment later by the shriek of two low-flying, Navy F-14 Tomcats.

There was a hiss as Rod reached up and broke the helmet seal at his collar. He removed the helmet and cradled it under his arm, looking down at Drake with cold, gray eyes. "A question, Lieutenant."

"Shoot."

"About the trap . . . how did you know that there was one? I scanned the room before we entered. In retrospect, I now recognize clues to the existence of a concealed hole in the floor. There was an anomalous cool area outlined beneath the carpet, and there were traces of fresh sawdust in the corners of the room. But those clues were not sufficient to make me suspicious at the time. How did you know?"

Drake shrugged. "Let's just say I didn't buy Ferré's act."

"With the wounded man. What did he do wrong?"

"Nothing wrong . . . but the act wasn't in character. Look, according to what you told me, he tortured Benny Armitage, one of his own people, just to punish the guy for talking to us. According to the women at the Strand, he's been using the whole island's population for slave labor . . . and using the women to keep his troops happy. And Rutherford told us what he did to Betty Foss, just to convince the congressman that he meant business. It looked to me like Ferré was a thoroughgoing bastard, an animal who would do anything, who would *use* people in the most horrible ways, just to get what he wanted."

"You reasoned all of that out when we encountered him by the trap?"

"No. Let's just say it was . . . human intuition."

A Marine gunnery sergeant trotted toward where Rod and Drake were standing in front of the porch. Very slowly, making no sudden moves, Drake lowered the cement-caked mess of his Uzi to the ground, then held up his hands.

"I recognize your big friend here," the Marine said. "Who are you?"

"Lieutenant Drake. Operation SEA KING."

"Thank you, sir," the Marine said, saluting. "Thought it might be you . . . but you don't look much like your ID picture under all that gunk. Gunnery Sergeant Carlson, 1st Marine Force Recon."

"I'm glad to see you, Gunny." Drake jerked his thumb over his shoulder. "You'll find Congressman Rutherford and his wife in there, safe and sound. Up the stairs, follow the hall to the right. Second door from the corner. And watch it. The congressman is armed and might be a bit jumpy."

"Aye, aye, sir." The Marine looked Drake up and down once. "Uh, if the lieutenant wouldn't mind my saying so, he is a fucking mess. I'll have one of my men help you with your gear, sir."

Drake sighed. "I'd appreciate that, Gunny."

American Marines continued to drift out of the tropical sky.

◖᷍ Chapter Eighteen

THE BATTLE FOR PIRATE'S CAY lasted for less than an hour, and when it was over, eighty-two men had been rounded up, disarmed, and penned in a temporary holding camp set up on the beach. Members of the Bahamian police were on hand, already interviewing the residents of Pirate's Cay and taking statements.

The butcher's bill for the impromptu revolt on the island wasn't in yet, but civilian casualties had been light: two known dead so far, a handful of wounded who were being treated by corpsmen of the 1st Marine Recon Force. Casualties among the smugglers were heavy: forty dead and as many more wounded. Most of the dead could be credited to Rod and his XM-214. Most of the wounded were victims of the liberated populace, of the Marines, or of firefights between separate and confused bands of disorganized rabble, firing into one another by mistake.

Weston had arrived by chopper shortly after Drake had finished hosing himself off. "Trying for a court martial, are we?" was all he'd said when he found Drake and Rod at the Strand, surrounded by an enthusiastic crowd of liberated islanders.

"Who's talking about a court martial?" Sammy Barris had

thundered. He held a shotgun in massive hands. "If it wasn't for these two boys . . ."

"Hold it, hold it," Weston said, putting up his hands. "These two disobeyed orders . . . but they'll probably come out of it smelling like roses. It's damned hard to prosecute a couple of *heroes*." He sneered the word. "Even when they deserve getting the book thrown at them!"

Rod did not understand Weston's anger. Apparently, RAMROD's director had gone ahead and requested a Marine unit—not AUTEC's security company after all, but a full Recon Force out of Camp Lejeune, North Carolina—as soon as he'd lost contact with Drake. Weston later explained that he'd received word through the U.S. embassy in Nassau that the hostages on the cay had been rescued. He'd not known at the time whether the hostages included the Rutherfords or not. He did know that he couldn't abandon the RAMROD team, and that there were times when the niceties of diplomacy could not be granted a greater value than even one human life.

But if he felt that way, Rod reasoned, why was he talking about court martials and throwing books?

He did understand that the invasion had ignited a firestorm. Strident voices in Nassau and elsewhere were already referring to the "unprovoked invasion, a blatant violation of Bahamian sovereignty." Perhaps Washington was already looking for convenient scapegoats.

Rod still could not understand why some powerful and influential people seemed to value careers and prestige and the need to fix blame more than the need to identify a problem and get the job done.

Get the job done. They were doing just that now, an hour after the confrontation with Weston. A Navy Seahawk helicopter sped south, low over the water. To the right lay the deep blue emptiness of the Florida Straits; to the left the marshy and swamp-infested eastern shore of Andros Island. The helo was in close pursuit, its target a red and white cigarette boat, a twelve-meter-long wedge trailing a powerful wake as it bounced across the waves. The helo's pilot had already clocked the boat at 130 knots in what was obviously an all-out run for safety . . . probably to Cuba, which at that speed lay less than an hour to the south.

Three men were on board. Rod had used his telephoto vision to record their images. Two were thugs in Ferré's employ. The other was Carlos Ferré himself.

It was time to close this particular chapter of WHITE SANCTION.

"Hey, Rod?" Drake asked, shouting to be heard above the thunder of the helo's rotors. The two of them were standing in the open side door of the Seahawk, the wind lashing at them as they descended toward the aquamarine blur of the waves below. "Why do it this way? We could pop 'em all from here."

Rod looked at Drake and gave a grim smile. The SEAL had managed to wash off most of the wet cement, but his hair was still in wild disarray. "The WHITE SANCTION directives call for capturing the target if possible."

"Yeah, but they're not stopping," said the Navy chief who shared the Seahawk's cargo deck with them. He patted the M-16 he was cradling. The weapon was equipped with a telescopic sight mounted on its carrying handle. "You saw me put sixteen rounds into that speedboat of theirs. They just refuse to give up!"

"True. But there is another way."

"Look." Drake said. "That bastard's not worth getting killed for. Let's waste him."

Rod lifted his helmet, dropping it over his head and sealing the latches. "Let's see if we can make him answer for his crimes first." Spoken through the helmet's speakers, his voice dropped in timber, a menacing rumble.

Tightly gripping the air-sea rescue cable that was suspended from the winch arm on the Seahawk's starboard side, Rod stepped into the air.

Normally, the winch was used to pluck men from the sea. This time, it held the robot between the helicopter and the sea, sweeping him in astern of the cigarette boat like some martial vision, an armored black knight descending from the skies.

There was consternation among the three men in the cigarette boat. Ferré held a CAR-15 subgun to his shoulder, blazing away on full-auto, firing, as Rod had hoped, at him and not at the helicopter ten meters overhead. Bullets sparked and sang as they struck him in the legs, torso, and arm. There was a real danger. If the gunman decided to fire at the helo, he might bring it down and kill them all. If a stray round or ricochet severed the cable, Rod would plunge into the sea, and while the waters here were shallow, it would be a long walk across Andros Island to civilization.

The helo gained on the boat, sweeping lower. . . .

Rod's vision field was cluttered with angles and vectors, with glowing numerals giving range, speed, and angle of approach. The pilot of the cigarette boat was weaving now, cutting broad S-shaped paths of white froth in the water.

But the boat responded sluggishly compared with Rod's speed of electronic scanning and calculation. He judged the proper moment . . . and let go.

Plunging through five meters of thin air, Rod landed in the narrow well deck of the cigarette boat, crumpling the deck with the force of his landing. The bow of the long racer reared high out of the water and the stern nearly submerged. Humans and robot were thrown to the deck. There was sudden silence as the high-powered engine flooded, choked, and died.

Rod regained his feet as Ferré opened fire at point blank range, sending a stream of 9mm rounds slamming into his helmet. Rod reached through bullets that shrieked and yowled as they bounced off his arm, grasping the weapon's barrel, twisting it aside; there was an explosion that split breach and muzzle as a round exploded in the sealed chamber. Dazed, Ferré stumbled backward, dropping the shattered weapon as he clawed at his bloody face.

The boat's pilot swung a heavy wrench in an overhanded swing. Rod plucked the wrench from the man's fingers and fed it to him, through splintered teeth. The second thug died as Rod's hand smashed his skull.

Then he turned on Ferré.

"Don't kill me! Don't kill me!"

Rod's hand closed on the smuggler's collar and lifted him, feet kicking, off the deck.

He valued the sense that Drake referred to as human intuition. As it was, he couldn't tell if Ferré's evident terror was genuine or a put-on, a prelude to another trap. Still, there was little Ferré could do now, save possibly blow the cigarette boat and plunge both him and the robot into the sea.

The man's terror, the robot decided in a measured, calculating way, was almost certainly genuine.

"Mr. Speaker, it has been suggested that members of this government, including the President, at least one of our colleagues in the Senate, and several other respected members of the government and the intelligence community, be censured for their parts in the affair that culminated last week in the Bahamas. Mr. Speaker, honored colleagues, I am here today to tell you that such censure is, in no uncertain terms, both wrong and detrimental to the shape and course of the government of the United States."

Drake leaned back in the narrow seat high in the balcony above the House of Representatives. Rod sat on his right, looking human again in Civilian Mod and a neat, dark suit. Weston was on his left, wearing a long expression and a rumpled sport coat and tie.

Below, on the House floor, Clyde Rutherford stood behind a podium, addressing the dozen or so fellow congressmen attending the session. More important issues had already been debated and most of the members had departed, but Rutherford continued to deliver the words with measured power, speaking them for the record if not for the impact they would have on his fellow representatives.

"You will know by now," Rutherford continued, "that Carlos Ferré has been returned to the United States and charged with crimes against American citizens ranging from conspiracy, kidnapping, assault and piracy to narcotics smuggling, terroristic threats, rape, and murder. That this monster who sought to undermine our society, to corrupt our government has been extradited to face justice in the United States is due entirely to the committee which the House seeks to have dismantled, to Group Seven and its remarkable technological offspring, Project RAMROD.

"The men and women of RAMROD, ladies and gentlemen of the House, are heroes, not criminals. I myself was Ferré's prisoner. He dared to reach out and paint me with his own, foul brush, to try to force me to comply with his wishes in this House. I am ashamed to say that it was not through any strength of character or resistance on my part that I was able to escape to address you here today. It was thanks solely to the members of RAMROD who, for security reasons, must remain unsung heroes.

"We have, all of us, seen the results of the drug plague that has racked this country. We have seen that better law enforcement is not, by itself, an answer to this plague. We have seen that increased spending on the antinarcotics bureaucracy is not the answer. We have seen that better education, while vitally important, cannot of itself be the answer. We have seen that campaigns such as 'just say no,' while they help cut the number of our children who experiment with drugs, cannot reduce the estimated tens of millions of people in this nation who are already hooked on cocaine, on crack, on heroin, on the new and deadly 'designer drugs' that are appearing on our streets in unprecedented numbers.

"I would like to put a question to this august body. Why, in light of continued failure in all of our efforts to fight the drug war, why do we seek to dismantle the one program that lets us strike back at the drug lords who are orchestrating the piece-by-piece, hit-by-hit destruction of this country? RAMROD, ladies and gentlemen, has the drug lords on the run, from Hong Kong to Colombia, from Thailand to New York. They fear RAMROD . . . and, I can assure you, they fear RAMROD with very great reason."

Drake listened to the words, but he knew it was too late. The full House vote would be tomorrow, and too many of the representatives, according to Clyde Rutherford, had already made up their minds.

The President had already made a formal apology to the Prime Ministers of both the Bahamas and Great Britain for the military incursion on Pirate's Cay. Officially and publicly, the "invasion" was a training exercise, part of the annual NATO Springboard exercises in the Caribbean. The story was that the landing on Pirate's Cay, due to some bureaucratic oversight, had not been properly cleared with the governments in Nassau or London. Few of the details had been released to the press, and there were hopes in the Pentagon, on Capitol Hill, and in the White House that the whole incident would blow over in reasonably short order.

But Weston's neck was still on the chopping block for

arranging for the incursion through his military contacts at the Pentagon and Camp Lejeune in the first place. Several military careers were in jeopardy as well . . . and Drake had already been told that his future as a commissioned officer in the Navy was finished. The question of criminal charges was still being discussed at various levels within the government, and no one had yet addressed what for Drake was the biggest question of all.

What would happen to RAMROD, and to the combat robot he knew as Rod?

Rutherford struck his podium with a clenched fist. "*No,* ladies and gentlemen of the House! We should not condemn this project, these people who have done so much for us in this war! Rather, we should condemn those among ourselves who have already surrendered, who have sold out their country to a foe no less menacing, no less evil than any dictator or enemy nation or twisted foreign creed in this nation's history! The enemy is not RAMROD. Our enemies are those who accept the evil as a necessary part of doing business . . . or for reasons of greed, or fear, or apathy!"

Drake turned again and found Rod looking back at him through emotionless, gray eyes. "I confess to some interest in the fate of Project RAMROD," he said. "And my personal fate as well."

"They can't do anything to us, Rod," Drake whispered. "We're *heroes,* remember?"

But he knew the unsteadiness of his voice was giving the lie away to Rod's keen hearing and powerful vocal stress analyzers.

"Not in the eyes of the majority of the House representatives," Rod said softly.

Operation WHITE SANCTION had already been declared illegal. The United States government could not ever, *ever* conduct assassination programs against foreign nationals, either in the United States or within the borders of other nations. It could not conduct military operations within other countries, or violate international borders with covert forces, for whatever reason.

The laws were crystal clear. The Buchanan Report, which predicted chaos and collapse within a few years if the drug plague went unchecked, was one man's opinion, not law . . . and it could never serve as an excuse for the government to violate its own principles.

Bullshit, Drake thought with a vehemence that surprised him. Survival of the fittest governed nations no less than animals in the wild. What good was international law, conventions of behavior, even civilization itself when the warlords who controlled the world's narcotics didn't recognize the same law, the same conventions, the same principles of civilization? The United States of America was being destroyed by an insidious enemy, assaulted from within and without . . . and her survival depended on her ability to fight back.

But more than one member of "this august body," as Rutherford called it, had already sold out to the enemy. Ferré had been carrying phone numbers on him when Rod captured him, and the investigation was already uncovering surprising connections to the international drug trade right here on Capitol Hill. It was a scandal of epic proportions . . . and it was already being covered over. Tomorrow, the final vote would come, officially condemning Group Seven and RAMROD, and directing that the individuals responsible be formally charged with crimes ranging from conspiracy to repeated violations of the Neutrality Act.

And what about Rod? What rights did a machine, a walking, thinking *computer* have under the law?

"We must fight this menace that has us by the throat!" Rutherford declared. "Fight drugs a kilo at a time and we'll drown in the drug lords' poisons. We must strike the head, not the body. We must strike the drug lords on their own home ground!"

"Let's get out of here," Weston said. "I can't listen to any more."

Silently, the three rose and made their way out of the visitors' gallery.

Perhaps, Drake thought, it was already too late. Perhaps the corruption had spread too far.

Outside the gallery, they were met by Senator Buchanan, who locked eyes with Weston and raised questioning eyebrows. "As expected?"

"The air in there is colder than Siberia, Senator," Weston said. "They're going to crucify us."

"Come on," Buchanan said. "All of you. There's someone outside who wants to talk to you."

They walked out of a side door and down endless steps outside. It was late in the evening already, and the lights of Washington were coming on.

A limousine was standing in a VIP waiting zone off Independence Avenue.

As an anonymous man held the rear car door for him, though, Drake realized that this was one fight he could never turn his back on. He had too much invested—of himself, of the people he worked with.

And there was Rod. He couldn't allow anything to happen to the machine who had become his friend.

It was an impossible battle. He knew that . . . but whether or not it was *possible* had very little to do with whether or not he should keep on fighting.

Weston got into the front passenger's seat, while Rod and Drake slid into the back. Someone was already in the back seat, waiting for them.

With a shock, Drake recognized the President of the

United States. "So you're Cybernarc," the President said, turning to look at the robot."

"RAMROD Mark I, sir," the robot replied. "I'm pleased to meet you."

"I'm impressed," the President said. He looked at Drake. "Lieutenant? We have to talk. About you, about Cybernarc here . . . and about the future of this country."

Drake felt a new surge of hope.

Perhaps they'd manage to keep the fight going after all.

🔊 *Epilogue*

THE WARM, BAHAMIAN SUN beat down on the streets of Windsor as Rod and Drake got out of their car and walked the short distance toward the Royal George. A smiling woman waved to them from a shop. Some fishermen working on their nets at the dock whistled and flashed a V-for-victory sign. Drake grinned and waved back, then stepped into the cool darkness of the pub.

"What'll you have?" Drake asked the robot as they walked up to the bar. "Oil? A two-twenty-volt pick-me-up?"

"I receive adequate recreation watching you imbibe various mild systemic poisons," the robot replied. "Thank you."

"You're welcome." He ordered a Goombay Smash. Sammy Barris, as always, refused to take his money.

The news from Washington was not good. House and Senate probes into the alleged improper activities of various elected officials had uncovered little: a House representative who admitted taking a little coke or marijuana now and then years ago, before he came to Washington, and a senator who'd confessed to sharing cocaine with a couple of pretty Senate pages at his suburban Maryland home. House and Senate ethics committee panels were proceeding with their investigations, but it was clear that the real deals—the laundered money schemes and the payoffs and kickbacks from drug lords and smugglers—were all being hidden under several metric tons of grade-A Washington manure.

And, ominously, Carlos Ferré had held a news conference at which he'd claimed that the system would never bring him to trial, that bucks were stronger than any jailhouse bars.

Ordinary men, it seemed, were too easily corrupted by money.

But the fight went on—for Rod because he was a machine, literally incorruptible; for Drake because he was not an ordinary man. He had reasons to see justice done that transcended any need for money, power, or a millionaire's life-style.

And there were incorruptible men in Washington, as well. Weston remained at the CIA, officially under reprimand, but in fact running his old desk in Global Issues, tracking the flow of narcotics across the world. And there was Frank Buchanan, and the President.

RAMROD no longer existed . . . not officially. But the inhabitants of Pirate's Cay had agreed to accept a technological research grant from the Rand Corporation . . . and the villa at Vista del Mar was being rebuilt from the ground up as a U.S. government research installation. Theoretically, the institution was studying global warming, but RAMROD Mobile One was parked in a brand-new hangar at the airfield with its recently extended airstrip, and local construction workers spoke among themselves of the size of the underground facilities "up the hill." Many of RAMROD's technical personnel had already taken up residence in some of the houses along the cay's southern and eastern coasts, houses that had been purchased or extorted by Ferré's men and had remained vacant for years.

The island, long held at the point of death by drugs and

terror, was coming alive once more.

And so as far as Drake and Rod were concerned, the fight went on. Group Seven continued to operate in Washington as a highly clandestine gathering of intelligence and drug-enforcement personnel answering through Senator Buchanan to the President.

And RAMROD continued to function out of Pirate's Cay, but as a covert operational group unknown to all but a trusted handful of people in Washington.

It could never have been any other way. Washington was the world's center for power, for politics, and for money; it was inevitable that the drug lords would insinuate their tentacles into that city.

RAMROD had gone underground, illegal, covert . . . but desperately needed. Buchanan's clock was running, and there wasn't much time left. If that meant they would break the law to hold back that remorseless ticking, then so be it.

Drake leaned against the bar and watched the other people in the Royal George. Angie Preston was at a table with her husband Bill. She grinned and waved, and Bill Preston hoisted his mug in salute. Elsewhere, people talked, laughed . . . lived.

"It was worth it, Rod," he said, speaking so softly that only the robot's sensitive ears could pick up the words.

"Indeed," Rod murmured. "Sometimes it is necessary to see the fruits of victory to make the fight worthwhile."

"Roger that."

"But I do wonder if we—the two of us—can make any real difference. Carlos Ferré was one of thousands. There are millions of addicts. Drugs continue to enter the United States. It seems unstoppable."

Drake sipped his drink and considered the question. More than once on this op, they'd demonstrated how perfectly the two of them complemented each other, Drake with his intuition, his caring, his driving, inner sense of purpose; and Rod, incorruptible, unswerving, relentless . . . and tainted somehow with an almost human sense of justice.

They were the perfect team, and together they would continue dealing death to the death dealers, for as long as it took to get the job done.

Charlie Mike. Continue Mission.

And hang the odds.

Drake grinned and gestured toward the people in the room. "Take a good look at them, Rod," he said. "We *did* make a difference, right here. With them. It doesn't get any clearer than that."

They would continue the fight.

Robert Cain in the pseudonym of an author who lives in Pennsylvania.

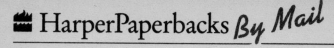